Duffle Bag Cartel

Lock Down Publications and Ca$h
Presents
Duffle Bag Cartel
A Novel by *Ghost*

Duffle Bag Cartel

Lock Down Publications
P.O. Box 870494
Mesquite, Tx 75187

Visit our website @
www.lockdownpublications.com

Copyright 2019 Duffle Bag Cartel

First Edition April 2019
Printed in the United States of America

This is a work of fiction. Names, characters, places, and incidents either are products of the author's imagination or are used fictitiously. Any similarity to actual events or locales or persons, living or dead, is entirely coincidental.

Lock Down Publications
Like our page on Facebook: Lock Down Publications @
www.facebook.com/lockdownpublications.ldp
Cover design and layout by: **Dynasty Cover Me**
Book interior design by: **Shawn Walker**
Edited by: **Tammy Jernigan**

Stay Connected with Us!

Text **LOCKDOWN** to 22828 to stay up-to-date with new releases, sneak peaks, contests and more…

Thank you.

Submission Guideline.

Submit the first three chapters of your completed manuscript to <u>ldpsubmissions@gmail.com</u>, subject line: Your book's title. The manuscript must be in a .doc file and sent as an attachment. Document should be in Times New Roman, double spaced and in size 12 font. Also, provide your synopsis and full contact information. If sending multiple submissions, they must each be in a separate email.

Have a story but no way to send it electronically? You can still submit to LDP/Ca$h Presents. Send in the first three chapters, written or typed, of your completed manuscript to:

LDP: Submissions Dept
Po Box 870494
Mesquite, Tx 75187

DO NOT send original manuscript. Must be a duplicate.

Provide your synopsis and a cover letter containing your full contact information.

Thanks for considering LDP and Ca$h Presents.

DEDICATION

This book is dedicated to my precious, beautiful Baby Girl, the love of my life, 3/10. That for always riding for me. You're my world.

ACKNOWLEDGEMENTS

I would like the thank the Boss Man and C.E.O of LDP, Cash. Thank you for this opportunity. Your wisdom, motivation and encouragement are appreciated. Thanks, Bruh.

To the Queen and C.O.O of LDP, thank you for all that you do, Sis. Your hard work, dedication and loyalty to this company never goes unnoticed.

The grind is real. The loyalty in this family is real. I'm riding with LDP 'til the wheels fall off. The GAME IS OURS!

Ghost

Chapter 1

Phoenix

"Ssh. Hurry up and come on." I whispered, taking Alicia by the hand and pulling her into the back of the stretch Navigator Limousine.

Alicia allowed me to. She hurried inside, after taking one quick glance over her right shoulder back to the house that she shared with my right-hand man. "Phoenix, you tripping. I know damn well you ain't got on yo mind what I think you do." She took a tuft of her short curly hair and placed it behind her ear, settled into the back seat of the limousine and looked me over closely. Alicia was five feet seven inches tall, light skinned and every bit of a hundred and forty pounds, thick. She had more ass than a donkey. Her small breasts, in my opinion, complemented her frame perfectly.

I rolled up the partition after telling the driver that we needed fifteen minutes before we headed to the church where Alicia was set to marry my homeboy. I slid closer to her, and placed my hand in her thick thigh, squeezed it, and rubbed slowly in between her legs. "Lil one you already know what it is. You about to marry my nigga today, but before you do I gotta hit this pussy one more time. Its only right. Now open these legs." My fingers grazed over the crotch of her lace panties. Her warm sex lips poked through them. That was another thing about Alicia, she had one of the fattest pussies that I'd ever seen in all of Memphis. I could never get enough of doing the most to it.

She tried to squeeze her thighs together. "Nall Phoenix. This ain't right. Mikey about to be my husband now. We

can't keep doing this behind his back. I don't feel right."
She tried to pry my hand from her thigh.

I pushed it away and slid it back toward the opening of
her short skirt. Those red thighs looked so tantalizing. For
me there was nothing like a thick woman. "That's why I
volunteered to pick you up so we can handle this bidness
for the last time. After y'all got married and I ain't trying
to hit this pussy no more, you got my word on that. Now
stop playing wit me." I pulled her thighs apart and dropped
to my knees in front of her, pulling her skirt all the way
back. The heavy aroma of her sweet smelling perfume
coming from between her legs, invaded my nostrils.

Alicia arched her back, opening her thighs as wide as
they could go. "Damn Phoenix. You always doing this kind
of shit Mane. I just wanna be faithful to my man. That's it."

I yanked them panties to the side and kissed along her
slit. Stopped and looked up to her. "Its good shawty, you
gon be able to do all of that from here on out. Trust me.
Just right now I need some of this pussy for old times sake."
My thumb spread her lips, exposing her pink. She moaned
deep within her throat and closed her eyes tight. I licked up
and down her glistening crease, making figure 8's around
her clitoris, and then sucking it into my mouth, darting my
tongue back and forth across it.

She held the side of my face and humped into me.
Wrapped her thighs around my neck, breathing heavy.
"Un. Un. Phoenix. Aw fuck baby."

She bucked. Yelped. "Phoenix. Phoenix. This is fucked
up. This is fucked up. I'm cumming. I'm cumming!" She
yelled, cocking her thighs open, cuffing her small titties in
her hands. I could see the hard nipples poking through the
material. It looked so good.

Her juices slid down my neck, and into my shirt. I could taste her on my tongue. As soon as I felt her shaking like crazy, I sucked her clit harder, making her run. She fell to the floor of the stretch. "Nall, get yo ass back here lil one." I picked her up and forced her knees to her chest. Had my dick outside of my pants in seconds running it up and down her dripping crease. Took the head and slid in, then slammed all nine inches home until my nuts were laying against her ass cheeks.

"Uhh." She gasped. "Damn you Phoenix. Damn you." The Limo rolled over a speed bump.

"For old times sake baby. That's all. Just for old times' sake." I slid my piece in and out of her, digging deeper and deeper with each thrust. Her tight, wet walls sucked at me with each stroke, the pussy getting better and better.

It didn't take long before her nails were scratching up my back, digging into my skin. "You fucked up, Phoenix. Aw. Shit. You so fucked up." She squeeze her eye lids together tightly as she laid the side of her face on the seat, a slight trace of drool sliding from the corner of her mouth.

I couldn't help slamming into that box hard, repeatedly. I was trying to knock them walls loose, especially if this was going to be my last time hitting this pussy, and out of love for my homeboy I was sure that it would be. Back in the day, when I was just thirteen, Alicia had been the first girl that I'd freaked. She moved away to New York for seven years, before coming back and becoming an item with my right-hand man Mikey. We'd all gone to school together. Her and Mikey had always had a thing for one another, and were considered an item from the ninth grade, all the way up and through our senior year.

Three years ago, he'd started going back and forth to New York to make a bunch of drop offs and pick ups.

While out there, he and Alicia rekindled what they always had back in high school and were now set to be married. I couldn't understand how any dude could allow for himself to be locked down by one female when there were so many bad bitches in the world, but to each their own. As long as I could get ahold of her whenever I wanted to, I didn't see a problem with it. Now that they were getting married, it was in my best interest to fall back and be considerate. Alicia's pussy was so good though. I felt her nails dig into my back, and trail down it. "Uhhhhh!" She hollered, shaking for the second time.

In and out.

In and out.

My piece slid back and forth through her lower lips. I could hear a constant sloshing sound. The pussy got wetter and wetter. Faster and faster I stroked, sucking her spiked nipples through her blouse, before pressing her knees further to her chest. I felt my seed getting ready to spill out of me. "I'm bout ta cum Alicia." More pounding. Faster and harder. "I'm bout ta cum shawty. Fuck!" I sucked on Alicia's neck. My hips crashed into her middle again and again. I was trying to knock them walls loose, as usual.

"Stop. Stop. Uh fuck, you killing my pussy! You killing it. Aw fuck yes! Un!" She threw her head back and came all over my pipe for the third time, triggering my orgasm. Her mouth wide open. "Aw. Aw. Yes Phoenix. Shit."

Five hard pounds later I began to jerk, cuming harder then I could remember. The session ended with me sucking all over her neck, I was careful to not leave any passion marks.

Alicia slowly slid from under me and put her panties back in place. "Damn Phoenix, you always making me do shit I don't wanna do. Shit I don't try to do. Now what if he get between my legs tonight, because it is going to be our honey moon, and my flower is still open the way it is? Damn you ain't right." She shook her head and pulled her skirt as far over her thighs as she could.

I took a wet wipe and ran it all over my dick, and sack below. Once I dropped Alicia off, I'd have to jump in the shower anyway before I got fresh and met Mikey at the church for the wedding. We were set to wear matching Gucci tuxedos. Mikey had been my dude for ten years now, ever since 2009, back when we were in high school.

"Did you hear what I said Phoenix? What if he feels that you've been between my legs when he gets down there tonight? What am I supposed to tell him?"

"Shawty you tripping. You already know how that thang between yo legs work. That mafucka is loose right now from me doing my thing, and an hour later it'll be good again. We gon have to bank on that because what's done is done." I rolled down the back window to allow some of the sex smells to drift out of it. It was April of twenty nineteen and Memphis was already experiencing some form of a heat wave. That global warming shit had to be serious. It was ninety-five degrees outside already at eight in the morning.

She sat across from me and crossed her thick thighs. Folded her arms in front of her chest. "You ain't right Phoenix. We should have never done this. Damn I feel horrible."

I scoffed. Opened the refrigerator and pulled out a bottle of pink Sprite. I needed to slow some shit down right away and wasn't nothing like that codeine. I took a nice swallow, and felt the syrup course down my throat, before it burned my belly. The heavy feeling came over me almost immediately. My eye lids felt like a ton of bricks. "Shawty, you came three times. Those are just the ones that I was able to feel. It didn't seem like you was experiencing no remorse when I was beating them guts in. Stop it with all them mafuckin dramatics. That shit over wit. Its time to get yo ass to the church so we can get you married." I laughed. It was hard not to. What type of woman fucked her soon-to-be husband's right-hand man hours before they got married? Memphis was something else and had been ever since I'd moved here from Phoenix, Arizona when I was ten years old.

"Shut up and let me taste that shit mane. I need a sip so I can ease my conscience. I don't know how I'm about to look my Fiancée in the eyes. Damn I'm bogus." I handed her the bottle. She took it and took a nice swallow from it, then gave it back to me. She wiped her mouth. "Phoenix, please, once we get married, please don't come at me like that no more. You know I got a weakness for you because of our history, but I really love Mikey. I wanna do right by him. He's a good man."

I took a long swallow from the bottle and rolled the window all the way down. There was a nice breeze that felt good on my face. The driver got on the highway and increased his speed. There were a couple cars that rolled past us blasting their music. I set my arm on the window sill. "You got my word. I think its cool that y'all tying the knot. Mikey really loves you, that's for real. Y'all just gotta stop arguing so much about every little thing. That shit ain't healthy."

"Yeah I know. No relationship is perfect, and I'm sure that our marriage won't be either. One thing I know for sure, that's that doing shit like this definitely won't help." She lowered her head and sighed. "Do you know that you're the only man that I've been with?"

14

I took another swallow and waved her off. "Stop playin wit me Alicia. I ain't trying to hear that bullshit. I already know that ain't the truth."

She shook her head vigorously. "No, I'm serious Phoenix, you're it. Me and him ain't even went all the way yet. I'm surprised he hasn't told you that yet."

I sat up, with my eyes bucked. "You saying this nigga about to wife you and he ain't even hit the pussy? Seriously?" I was shocked and in disbelief.

She nodded. "Yeah, we were waiting until marriage. I told him that I've only been wit one man though. I just never told him that the man was you. I'm pretty sure he'd kill my ass if he found that out. You already know how crazy Mikey is." She shook her head and took the bottle of Sprite from me and turned it up.

I felt bad. I didn't know that Mikey had never fucked Alicia. I figured that he was saving her as his own special lil piece and here it was that I'd been fucking her all along behind his back. I had to stop that shit. I needed to get better dick control, and more of a conscience because as it stood, I didn't have either. I loved pussy, and in my book no female was off limits. Turning pussy down was my problem.

"Alicia, it's all good, shawty. This our last time being together. I ain't gon allow you to fuck up your marriage wit my potna. Me and bruh thick as thieves. This shit gotta stop, so you ain't got nothin to worry about. That's my word."

She came across the aisle and sat beside me. Took my hand and interlocked our fingers. "Phoenix, there is something that I want you to know even before I get married. That's that I really do love and care for you. I need for you to know that. You are always going to be my weakness. That's why I'm asking you to cut me some slack once I say my vows today." She kissed the back of my hand and looked into my eyes.

"Damn Alicia. You already know I'm crazy about you. You're my first. Even though you marrying my potna them feelings gon always be there for you. You feel me?" I kissed the side of her forehead, and kept my lips pressed against it.

"Thank you for saying that Phoenix. I swear to God I needed to hear that." She took a deep breath and exhaled, falling against me. "Just be my big brother from here on out. I know I'm going to need you along the way.

***

If there is anybody in this church who knows why these two shouldn't be joined in holy matrimony speak now or forever hold your peace." The Pastor said, as he stood in front of them with his purple and gold robe. The Bible was opened in his hand.

The church was packed. On Alicia's side there were mostly her relatives from Queens, New York. They were dressed respectfully and looked well groomed. They wore expensive outfits that coordinated with the brides white and beige wedding dress. Across the aisle were Mikey's wedding guests. Most of them were dope boys. They were fitted in denim shorts, black tees, and plenty of gold jewelry, over Jordans and Airmax. Many of them were from Orange Mound. That was our projects. A place we called home.

I looked around to see if anybody was going to try and rain on my man's parade. The pastor waited for a full five minutes before he proceeded with the vows. Fifteen minutes later, Mikey and Alicia became husband and wife. I still couldn't believe it.

Chapter 2

When I was seventeen years old, my mother passed away from cervical cancer. She was the love of my life, and one of the only people in this world who gave me a reason to give a fuck about anything. After her passing my heart became colder than an ice cube in a freezer. That was until my daughter was born on March tenth of two thousand and eleven. She was eight years old and the new love of my life. Her name was Shantê. She had the same light caramel complexion that my mother once had, and the same hazel eyes, with light freckles. Her hair was bushy and fell to the middle of her back. She was my weakness.

Two weeks after Mikey and Alicia became husband and wife, my baby mother, Toya showed up at my crib in Orange Mound with my daughter at five in the morning. She beat on the door with her closed fist until I answered it in my boxers. I had my forty-five automatic in by right hand and my lip curled. I didn't even take the time to ask who the hell it was beating on the door. I simply threw it open and aimed the gun as soon as the door swung outward.

Toya jumped and pulled Shantê with her. "Boy what the fuck is you doing. Put that damn thang away before you hurt somebody!" Toya yelled.

Shantê yanked her hand from her mom's grasp and ran into my apartment, leaving her mother to fend for herself. She hugged my waist. "Daddy. Daddy. I missed you. I don't want to live wit my mama no more. Its boring, and she don't buy me nothin." She hugged me tighter and looked up at me with watery eyes.

I lowered my gun and rubbed her back. "Its okay baby. We'll figure it out, don't worry okay?"

She nodded. "Okay. But can I stay here wit you to-night?"

Toya brushed past me and stepped into the house. "I just got evicted. We ain't got nowhere to go, so I don't know what to tell you." She walked into the kitchen and opened the refrigerator. Toya took out an Apple juice and popped the top. Drinking it, staring at me.

I closed the door and locked it. After sliding the gun into the small of my back, I knelt in front of Shantê. "Baby, go in the back to daddy's room and get your I-pad. Play on it for a little while so me and mommy can talk. Make sure you close the door. Okay?"

She nodded, and then motioned with her finger for me to bend down. As soon as I did, she kissed my cheek. "I love you daddy. Please don't let mommy take me back to that house no more."

"Shantê get your ass into the back room! You're only eight years old. You do as you're told!" Toya snapped stepping toward her.

"Okay!" Shantê, jumped in fear and rushed toward the back room. She got inside and slammed the door. I could hear my baby crying through it. That pissed me off.

"Look Toya I don't know what you been doing to my baby, but you ain't finna be acting like you finna beat her or something. Clearly you got a lot going on at your place or she wouldn't be acting like that. Now how the fuck did you get evicted?"

She shrugged her shoulders, stepped into the living room and plopped on the couch with her head down. "I missed a few rent payments. Shit been kind of tight, and I just ain't had the money. That's the truth."

Toya was dark skinned with micro braids in her hair that fell just below her shoulders. She was about five feet three inches tall, a hundred and thirty pounds. Facially gorgeous. I'd met her in Orange Mound eleven years prior and it had been lust at first sight. We'd tried the relationship thing, but it didn't work. I was a street nigga at heart, and I loved pussy way too much to be tied down to one female. I just couldn't see it.

Irritated, I sat on the couch across from her. "What's up with that fool Bryon? I thought y'all was going strong?" Bryon had been her boyfriend for the last two years. He was one of those good dudes. That nigga had a nine to five working as a mechanic and all that good stuff.

"Me and Byron ain't talking no more. He back to messing wit one of his exes and I ain't about to play second fiddle to no bitch. I gotta be number one. But anyway, I need you to cop us a new apartment like a-sap and until then we gon stay right here with you. Deal wit it." She rolled her eyes.

"What make you think I got that kind of paper shawty?"

Toya laughed. "Phoenix stop playing wit me. Nigga I know you holding. All you do is trap. You and that fool Mikey. Y'all name ringing through the Mound like crazy. Aw you got it." She took another long swallow of the apple juice.

I mugged her and shook my head. "We about to be twenty-five soon Toya. When you gon get yo shit together?" I stood up and headed down the hallway. Placed my hand on the door to my bedroom.

Toya followed. "First of all, you making it seem like you're feeling some type of way because I brought me and our daughter here. We ain't got nowhere else to go. Secondly, I shouldn't have to raise her on my own no way. You out here doing all this fuckin hustling and we still living in the got damn projects. So, if anybody needs to grow

19

up its you." She spat. Her chest heaved up and down as if she was close to being out of breath. That was one of the reasons me and Toya couldn't be together. Her mouth and attitude was bogus. She knew how to hit all my buttons without really trying. While I cared about her because of my daughter, I had to take her in short doses. My temper was too horrible.

I turned around to face her. "Toya, there you go wit that slick ass mouth. Every time somebody say something to you, you got a habit of popping off at the tongue. If you gotta stay in my shit for a few weeks that ain't gon happen, or else I'm gon smack you in that mafucka. On every thang."

She smacked her lips. "Nigga please. You smack me and I'ma make you use that gun in the small of yo back, homeboy. I don't know what the fuck you think this is, but it ain't sweet." She frowned. Her upper row of teeth were capped with open faced golds.

"Look shawty, I ain't got no problem whooping yo ass. Just cause I ain't did it yet don't mean that I won't. I don't be letting hoes talk that bullshit to me. Straight up."

"I ain't no ho. You can stop that shit right now. I got yo muthafuckin daughter. That alone should make you refrain from calling me out of my name. Now respect me in honor of her at the very least." She mugged me.

I wanted to get at her but decided to let her have the argument, besides she was right to a certain extent. When I looked at her it was a must that I saw Shantê as well. "Well shawty you ain't staying here. I'ma about to get you right. Go sit yo ass down in the living room and I'll be in there in a minute. How much bread you think you need?"

She softened. "I don't know, a couple bands maybe. Whatever you can stand really." Toya attempted to give me her most winning smile. I wanted to muff her ass.

"Aiight, I'ma see what I got in here, and get at you in a minute. Gon chill on the couch." She walked off, and I stepped into my bedroom, and locked the door.

Shantê lay on her stomach playing Fortnite on her I-pad. When she heard the door close, she paused it and looked back at me. "Daddy you not about to make me go with her, again are you?"

I shook my head. "Nall baby you're good. I just gotta grab your mother a few pennies so she can get you guys another place to live. You ain't going nowhere tonight though. I promise."

"O-kay." She looked sad. "But do I gotta go some-where tomorrow wit her? Daddy, I don't like Bryon. He's so mean, and his whooping hurt too bad. He give me marks."

I was on my knees in the closet with a Jordan shoe box in front of me. Inside of it was ten thousand dollars. It was all I had to my name. At the mention of a grown ass man whooping my daughter I stopped, almost stuck in time. "What did you just say Shantê?"

"I said he whoop me too hard. It hurts. Plus, I got these things on my back that I saw in my mommy's tall mirror. They burn." She sat up and lowered her head.

I dropped the money back into the shoe box and stood up. "Baby hold your arms above your head. I'm about to take your shirt off so I can see your back."

"Okay." She got out of the bed, lifted her arms, and al-lowed for me to pull her shirt over her head. As soon as I saw the purple welts across her back, my vision went hazy. I started to shake. "Do you see them daddy?"

Across Shantê's back were reddish purple welts. About twenty of them. "Who did this to you baby? Did mommy do this?"

She shook her head. "No, mommy just smack me, then Bryon whooped me for a long long time with my clothes off. He's so mean daddy. I was crying for you, and he beat me harder. He said he my daddy and to shut up. She hugged my waist. "He hurt me so bad daddy." Now she was in full on tears and sobbing loudly.

I was so mad that all I could see was murder. "Baby, I promise you that Bryon will never put his hands on you ever again. In fact, you will never see him ever. I promise this to you. Do you hear me?" I knelt in front of Shante. Brushed her hair out of her face, then wiped away her tears with my thumbs.

She nodded. "Daddy, why are you shaking?"

That only made it worst. "I'm okay baby. I need you to get in the bed and play your game. Later, I'm going to take you over cousin Kamaya's house. Alright?"

She smiled. "I love her." She jumped into the bed and grabbed her IPad.

I counted out three gees and rolled it into a knot. A few minutes later I left the bedroom and stepped in front of Toya who was sitting on my white leather couch texting away on her phone. "Huh bitch." I took the bundle of money and threw it into her face as hard as I could. The money seemed to explode. It landed all over the living room.

She jerked her head back, covered her face with her hands, and dropped her phone. "What the fuck is wrong with you Phoenix?"

I grabbed a handful of her hair and threw her ass to the floor. "Punk ass bitch, you got some nigga putting his hands on my daughter!" She was about to say something, but I slapped her across the face, knocking her back to the floor.

She struggled to get up, came to her knees and held her mouth. "That's why I left his ass. Damn. You ain't got no right to be putting your hands on me Phoenix. You split my lip."

"Bitch." I grabbed her throat before she could retreat. Still enraged, I picked her up and held her against the wall. Her little feet kicked wildly while I choked her tighter and tighter. Then I dropped her to the floor like a rag doll.

Toya began to cough, crawling across the floor. She hawked and spit on the carpet. "I hate you Phoenix. I hate your fucking guts. You know I would never let nobody touch our daughter."

"Stand up bitch. Look me in my eye and tell me that shit. Tell me how long you been letting dude's bitch ass put his hands on my shawty? You better tell me before I go back in that room and ask my baby this same question, and bitch if she tell me anything that's the wrong thing, I'm finna slay you right here and right now. I pulled the gun out of the small of my back and cocked it, dead set on murdering my baby mother.

Toya held her throat and came to her feet, staggered, and breathed ruggedly. "He only beat her like four times. That's it. He be working so hard at that damn auto shop and sometimes Shanté can be so whiney. When he tell her to shut up, she always telling him that he ain't her father. That gets annoying."

I lost it and wound up slamming Toya against the wall so hard that she wound up putting a big ass dent inside of it. The plaster spilled onto the carpet. White smoke billowed into the air, choking us both. I coughed. "He ain't her muthafuckin daddy. And he ain't got no rights putting his filthy hands in my baby. She eight." I tightened my grip. "Where he at right now?"

Toya slapped at my hand, until I let her go. She sucked in a gasp of air. Coughing. Spitting on the carpet once again. "I'm sorry Phoenix. Don't choke me no more. Please." More coughing. "That nigga at work. He don't get off until eight o'clock tonight." She held her throat and swallowed.

I mugged her for a long time. "You finna roll out wit me to his crib and I'ma show you what happens to grown ass men that beat little girls. Especially when it's my little girl. Pick up that money and let's go."

I watched my baby mama crawl around on the floor, collecting one-hundred-dollar bill after the next. "Just let it go Phoenix. You don't need to go over there and do nothin to him. I already left his ass alone. He'll never hurt her again. Trust me." She gathered the last bill and stood up with tears sailing down her cheeks. Even though me and her weren't together I hated to see my baby mother cry. I know it didn't seem like it when I was choking her ass out over my daughter, but it was the truth.

"Toya, that shit ain't up to you no more. Its up to me. He put his hands on the wrong lil girl, now he gotta lay for that shit. That's how that's gone go. Now come on. I'ma drop Shantê off at Kamaya's crib and me and you about to go and handle this bidness." I grabbed her arm and pushed her toward the front door, just as there were four knocks that sounded upon it.

I quickly moved Toya out the way. "Who is it?" I hollered with a mug on my face.

"Its Kamya cuz. I need to holler at you about something important."

24

Duffle Bag Cartel

I smiled before opening the door to reveal all five feet four inches of my redbone cousin. She was my father's brother's daughter. Her mother was Italian. Kamya's long, jet black, curly hair, fell past her waist. Her eyes were light brown. She was slim up top, and down low she as built like a southern sista. Out of all my family Kamya was my favorite relative. We were closer than two fat chicks in a small elevator. I looked down to Toya. "Shid this even better. Kamya I need you to watch my daughter while me and Toya go handle this bidness. When I get back then me and you can holler. Aiight?"

She nodded. "You gon like the news I got too. Gimme my hug." She stepped into the house and wrapped her lil arms around my neck, kissing my cheek. Cuz smelled like Prada. Everything Kamya rocked was Prada. It had been that way since we were thirteen years old.

I broke our embrace and grabbed Toya's hand leading her out of the house. "Let's go shawty. Now."

Ghost

Chapter 3

We were parked a half of block away from Bryon's crib. We had been there for two hours with Meek Mill's Championship's playing out of the speakers of my Dodge Durango. Toya sat in the passenger's seat shaking like an earthquake. She glanced down the block over and over, then she'd stop and shake her head. "Man, I don't wanna do this Phoenix. If you fuck wit this dude its gon cause a world of trouble for us. He might not be in the streets, but he got six brothers that roll hard in Black Haven. They bout that life. I don't want nothin to happen to my baby daddy. You're all that me and Shanté have."

Just hearing her put so much power and fear into Bryon was pissing me off. I didn't like the fact that she appeared to be more afraid of what the back lash would be from what I was getting ready to do to him, instead of what he'd already done to my daughter. That was annoying to say the least. "Listen to me Toya. I don't give a fuck about dude, or his punk ass brothers out of Black Haven. He put his hands on my daughter. She got welts and all kind of shit all over her back from this grown ass nigga. I ain't finna let that shit ride. She's just a baby."

"She's eight Phoenix. Damn. And her mouth is too smart to be eight. Now she didn't deserve what he did to her, but maybe you need to talk to her about how she talk to adults and we wouldn't be in this mess. She don't listen to nobody but you. That's her problem." Toya said all of this with her body pressed against the passenger's door. She must have known that every word that she uttered pissed me off more and more. By the time she finished my heart was pounding, I wanted to snatch her black ass up.

I slid my leather gloves onto my hands and took the pistol from under my seat and put it on to my waist. "Nall that's you and his problem. Now bring yo ass on." I opened the door to my truck, got out and slammed it back, just as she did the same on the other side.

Toya lowered her head and took a deep breath. "You be doing too much Phoenix. Look at all these people out here. You don't think they gone remember us?" She said this with the sun shining from her forehead. It felt like it was close to a hundred degrees. There was a slight breeze, but it did very little to shelter one from the mounting humidity.

Looking around there were plenty people out on their porches already. Some were setting up barbecue grills. Others were watering their grass. A few were washing their cars. There were a group of six little girls that were jumping double Dutch just off the sidewalk. They were singing some nursery rhyme in time with their jumping. To my left was a group of young niggas. They were about eight deeps, all smoking on one thin ass blunt. I sized them up quickly and brushed their threat off. I had seventeen shots in my Glock. If need be, I would have used a bullet for each one of them, and still been left with nine. Out if the whole block they were the only threats I really saw, and if they were sharing a blunt between the eight if them, that meant they were broke in my eyes, and more then likely shared one pistol. Memphis was transparent like that.

I'd never saw Toya walk as slow as she did, getting to Bryon's house. We made it up his driveway. There was a rusty old pickup truck in it with an engine in the back. We got to the side of the house, and Toya stood there looking at me like I was stupid. Sweat slid down the side of her face.

"Shawty what you waiting on? I know you got a key to this bitch. Let's go." I urged looking over my shoulder. The neighborhood appeared to be going on about its business. More people were coming outside from what I could tell. That worried me some because I had plans on popping Bryon. I was gonna make sure that he never put his hands on my daughter again.

Toya pulled the keys out of her pocket and stepped up to the door. "Let me appeal to you one more time Phoenix. Please don't do this. He ain't mean to do what he did. I promise he won't ever do it again." Her bottom lip quivered.

I stepped up to the door and leaned into her face. "Toya, you testing my patience right now. Open that muthafuckin door and let me handle my bidness before I fuck you up first. Open the damn door, or I'ma kick that bitch in." I growled, getting more heated by the minute.

She sighed, and placed the key inside of the lock, then opened it. As soon as I saw it leave the door jamb, I pushed it all the way in and pulled out the Glock. I grabbed her and yanked her inside of the house as well. It smelled like bacon. I could hear something frying close by and I surmised that it was probably just that.

Grabbing Toya by the shirt, I made my way toward the kitchen with my gun leading the way. His house was mostly empty, as if he'd just moved in. Tori Lanez was bellowing from the speakers somewhere in the distance. I made my way closer and closer to the kitchen. When I was about twenty feet away, I could hear what sounded like a male voice singing along to the song. I let go of Toya and held my finger to my lips, motioning for her to get behind me. She followed my orders and covered her mouth. Five steps away. Then four. Three. The heavy scent of bacon

29

filled my nostrils. Toya stopped short and crouched down in the hallway. Tears were in her eyes again. She must have known what I was about to be on.

I rushed into the kitchen, just as Bryon was loading two plates of scrambled cheese eggs and pancakes with bacon. When he saw me, he dropped the skillet. Hot grease popped into the air. The skillet bounced off the floor and spilled its contents on to the linoleum. Before he could get a word out, I swung and smacked him so hard with the gun that he flew into the refrigerator and knocked the boxes of cereal from atop it. He fell on his side and jumped back up. "Say Mane, what's all this shit right here bout. Hopefully not dat bitch over thur." He pointed at Toya.

I kicked him as hard as I could in the ribs, then smacked him with the gun one more time. He fell to the floor. "You bitch ass nigga. You gon put yo hands on my muthafuckin daughter. Huh!" Another kick to the ribs.

He flipped on his back, and scooted away, holding them. "What? I ain't did shit to yo daughter mane. Her mama beat her ass, not me."

"Stand yo punk ass up." I ordered, aiming the gun at him.

"Nigga put that gun down and we can handle this like men. You come into my home on this bull shit. Let me see what you really got." He urged, breathing hard.

"Stand yo punk ass up nigga. Hurry up or I'm bout to pop you!" I cocked the hammer and aimed at his face.

He slowly made his way to his feet. There was a serious mug painted on his face. Bryon was every bit of six feet four inches tall. He had to weigh in at two fifty. He looked all muscle too. I was six feet even, about a hundred and eighty pounds, slim, and muscular. His skin was black as oil. His eyes a yellowish red. Compared to my light caramel complexion, he made me look almost white. I was good wit my hands, but his size was intimidating. I knew my bullets would break him down to size real quick.

"Ain't nobody did nothin to yo baby gurl mane. Some body lying on me. Can't be nobody but yo baby mama. She just mad cuz I ain't fuckin wit her like that no mo. Bitch is a bum."

Toya walked into the kitchen. "I tried to prevent this. I begged him to not get in yo ass Bryon, and all you've done is disrespected me this whole time. Now I don't care what he do." She said this and walked up on him.

"Bitch you lying anyway. I ain't never touch that man's shawty. You beat that baby every day. Not me."

"You're lying!" She tried to push him as hard as she could, right in the chest.

He grabbed both of her wrists. Pulled her back to him and smacked her so hard that he knocked her out. "Stupid ass bitch." He looked down on her and kicked her in the stomach.

I lost my breath. My eyes damn near popped out of my head. The shock caught me off guard so bad that he wound up punching me in the jaw before I could block it. The punch hurt so bad that everything went black for a second. I came to and he was dumping on my back. *Whom.* The pistol fell out of my hand and slid across the floor.

"You wanna come at me in my crib about that lil bitch! Then tell her to watch her fucking mouth!" A kick to my ribs flipped me onto my back.

I laid there for a second trying my best to catch my breath. Byron raised his steel toe boot to stomp me in the face. I rolled out of the way and jumped up. A sharp pain shot through my ribs. My arms wrapped around his waist and I picked him up in the air, before I fell backward wit him. His head ricocheted off the stove and busted open. Suddenly he was on his back hollering in pain with blood running down his neck.

"You muthafucka. You bitch ass muthafucka." He found his footing.

We met in the middle of the kitchen, throwing blows like savages. One of mine caught him in the jaw and rocked him. At the same time one of his slammed into my ear lobe. That shit hurt. I wasn't trying to feel another one of them. He swung a haymaker that followed that one. I ducked it and came back up and hit him with a right cross. Blazed him. His nose cracked. A head butt sent him flying backward. I chased him with blow after blow. My knuckles pounded into his face back to back. By the time it came to the third blow he was dizzy. His knees got weak. He hit me with another weak blow. I shook it off, and kept on swinging, fucking him up. He fell to his knees, sleep. I grabbed the sides of his head and slammed my knee into his face as hard as I could. Blood spattered around it. He laid against the refrigerator snoring.

I rushed and grabbed the pistol from the hallway floor, and drug him into the middle of the kitchen. Laid him on his back and proceeded to beat him over the face with the gun over and over. Harder and harder. "Nigga. Don't. You. Ever. Put. Yo. Muthafuckin. Hands. On. My. Daughter. Or. My muthafuckin. Baby. Mother. Again. Bitch. Nigga." Blow after blow was delivered until his face caved in on one side. When I felt that he didn't have any chance of getting up, I stood, and looked down at him. The entire kitchen floor was covered with his blood. It looked like a scary movie.

Toya staggered over to me and looked down. "Oh my God. Phoenix, what did you do? What did you do?" She started to walk over to him and slipped twice in the blood. Caught her balance and knelt in the blood before him and placed two fingers on his neck. She held them there and searched all around. Her eyes got more and more bucked. Then she sat back on her haunches and shook her head. "He gone Phoenix. This nigga is gone. What are we gone do?"

My jaw and my ear were killing me. Both were ringing like crazy. I didn't give a fuck about that nigga being dead. As far as I'm concerned at least I wouldn't have to worry about him putting his hands on my daughter again. I felt like pissing on him. "It is what it is. Get yo ass up out of that blood. I'm bout to call Mikey so we can get rid of this clown."

"But all of them people are outside Phoenix. What if they say something?" Toya asked standing up, and once again slipping on the blood. She sashayed across the floor as if she were skiing until she was standing in front of me. Her top lip was swollen.

I rubbed the side of her face. "Don't worry about that shawty. Me and bruh gon handle this bidness here. I'ma drop you back off in Orange Mound." I pulled her to me and wrapped her in my arms. I looked down at Bryon and felt nothin but anger. "Yeah shawty I got this."

Ghost

Chapter 4

Mikey grunted, as he helped me to hoist Bryon's body on to the slab inside of his uncle David's Funeral home. It was located ten blocks from Orange Mound. The door to the oven of the cremation machine was already opened. I could feel the intense heat coming from it. It smelled like gasoline and burnt skin from the past cremations. I felt weird being inside of David's Funeral home and did every time I came inside of his joint.

Mikey straightened Bryon's body, and started the conveyor belt that would send him into the flames. He was five feet eleven inches tall, caramel skinned like me, and just as muscular. He had a low-cut Mohawk that was tapered on the sides. When it came to getting rid of bodies, he was a beast. His uncle David was a mortician and funeral home director. Before that he was a straight street nigga and got down in the slums. He taught Mikey some of the tricks of his trade, and because he had, we'd already stripped Bryon naked per the orders of David. I watched his body slowly travel the path to the oven. "I bet dirty ain't never think his ass a be cremated before the day was out." He laughed, looking over at me. "I wish I would have been there. I would have done the same thing that you did. Shantê is my God daughter. I'd kill a million niggas over her." He frowned and slapped Bryon's naked chest before he was fed to the fire. His skin began to pop and crackle loudly. Once his whole body was fed into the flames, Mikey closed the oven's door, and took his big, black gloves off. "There, that shit is done. Now let's get on something new. I got some shit I wanna run by you Potna. Come upstairs." He took one last look over his shoulder, and then we were headed up the back stairs that led to one of his many apartments.

When we got to the top of the flight of the narrow hallway, he beat on the door, after trying the knob. "Dis damn gurl always locking the doe Durty. Dat shit get on my nerves like a mafucka." He beat on it again, louder this time. "Alicia open the got damn doe shawty. Fuck you in thur doing?"

I shook my head and laughed. "Nigga how the fuck can you sleep above a funeral home? Don't you be having nightmares and shit?" I wondered. The heavy aroma of burnt corpse and embalming fluid was in the air.

"Mane don't shit make me have nightmares other than being broke. Long as I got my cake up like birthday parties, I'm good to go Durty."

Alicia opened the door, fitted in a tight pink and black robe. Her hair was wrapped in a bath towel. "Damn bae, you beating like you're the police. Got me in thur scared as hell. I almost ran to your stash and started flushing shit." She rolled her eyes and turned to walk away.

He smacked her on her big ass and pulled her into his embrace, kissing all on her neck. "Dats how you gon talk to a boss shawty. You gon make me spank that ass in front of my mans. Dat what you want?" He asked sucking on her neck some more.

She laughed and tried her best to get away from him. "I'm sorry baby. Damn. Nall I don't want no spanking right now. You just scared me that's all." Alicia laughed some more, then ran from him. The back of her robe flying upward to reveal that fat caramel ass. The cheeks jiggled.

Mikey smiled, and shook his head. "I had to marry her lil thick ass. I'da been a damn fool not to of."

Duffle Bag Cartel

I felt my piece hardening just thinking about the last time I'd smashed Alicia. Her pussy was always good especially from the back. Them cheeks were soft and felt so delightful crashing into my lap. I shook myself out of my zone. "Y'all make a perfect couple Mane. What good wit this bidness though?"

Mikey waved for me to follow him down the hallway. His crib was nicely furnished, with hardwood floors. Now that I was inside of it, it smelled like incense. That was cool. That funeral home scent was horrible. We wound up in the guest bedroom. He closed the door behind me and motioned for me to sit on the couch. "You just plant yo ass right thur and I'm about to show you something. That two-liter bottle of Sprite got a sixteen in it. Pure codeine. Take you a shot of dat shit homeboy." He opened the closet door.

He ain't have to tell me twice. I twisted the cap and filled the glass that was already on the table. "Dis glass clean ain't it?"

Mikey grabbed a duffle bag and carried it to the couch, then sat down on it. "Yeah I bought that glass in here right before you called me earlier. I was gon turn up and take my wife down, but you said you needed me, so I put that shit on the back burner. You good nigga."

"Cool." I filled the glass, and swallowed half of it. That codeine was stronger than Popeye on his spinach. It burned my throat and gave me that sleepy effect right away. I fought through it and allowed myself to lean like somebody with a broke hip. In a matter of minutes, I was feeling kosher. High as heaven, eyes low as hell.

Mikey unzipped the duffle bag and pulled out a Mach Ninety. He set it on the table and set two clips beside it. Then he pulled out another one with the same number of clips. "These bitches scream three bullets at a time and hold

37

eighty in the clip. Both got scopes on top of 'em. We can buck a nigga down from across the street, or down the block. They got an accuracy level of eighty five percent. You can't beat that when it comes to a fully automatic. But I ain't done." He dug around in the bag and came up with two fully automatic forty fives. Then bruh put clips beside them that looked liked oversized Pez dispensers. He screwed a silencer into one of them. "Mafuckas ain't ready for these bitches here mane. Fully automatic forty fives that spit with ninety five percent accuracy. Military edition. Silenced. These bitches keep secrets that only we gon know about." He laughed and tossed one of them to me. "That's yours, and so is that Mach right thur."

That was just like Mikey, no matter what bro did he always made sure that I was just as good as he was. He was a good nigga. I had mad love for him, despite what had taken place with me and Alicia. "This good looking bruh, but now that we got these tools what you tryna do? You got something on your mind?"

He grabbed the bottle of Sprite and turned it up. "Don't I always." He took three long swallows, before setting it down. "Dragon nem. Them fools right down the way from Orange Mound. Its time we take a good look at them. We need that turf if we gon really kick this Duffle Bag shit off the right way. I got some of my cousins that's coming down from Brooklyn next month. By the time they touch down I wanna have everything in place. Its time we get all our ducks in a row. You feel me Mane?"

I felt like my eye lids were heavy as anvils. "I got seven gees to my name, and a daughter. My baby mama just got evicted from her crib, and as much as I care about her I ain't trying to have her living wit me bruh. I need my space.

That mean I gotta get her right. Its time I start to take care of my ladies, bruh. That's what's real."

"Yeah well I hear that. On some real shit we can bring this city to its knees, Phoenix. I got a crazy plug out in Brooklyn that a hit me wit whatever to sew this bitch up, but before we do that, we gotta move some niggas around, and snatch they clientele. What's crazy is while I'm doing all of this I still gotta finish these last few credits so I can get my business degree. I found three buildings. One gone be a barber shop for the lil homies to work out of. Another one gone be a beauty salon for the women, and I'ma put my mother's restaurant in the other one. She been dying to put that Creole food out there for a long time in such a way. So, we gotta get a move on. You know what you wanna do outside of this street life shit?"

I looked the forty-five over in my hand. It looked so pretty. I could imagine sparks flying from the barrel as I bucked something down. "Nall, I don't know what I wanna do yet. Like I said before I only got seven gees to my name. So, I don't feel right. I can't see that far into the future right now. I gotta take care of my daughter today. That's all that matters to me."

Mikey nodded. "I can feel that my nigga. You already know what's mine is you're. Its gone always be that way. I ain't got no shorties yet, but Shantê is my heart. I gotta help you get right so you can make sure she's good at all times." He grabbed a blunt from his front pocket and sparked it. A thick cloud of gray smoke appeared and floated toward the ceiling. "I got this move I want us to bust for a friend. First, we gone bust the move, then I'ma introduce you to who the move was for."

"How much we talking?" I asked. I didn't give a fuck who the move was for, it had to be beneficial to me at the same time.

"Its for ten gees total. We can split the pot fifty fifty. That'll push you up to twelve. If all goes right this one favor is going to put us in to the path of a hundred more. Before the summer get here, we should be sitting lovely and well on the way to starting our Duffle Bag Cartel. Cuz nem from Brooklyn have already said they're down for the cause. They got a lot of heat back East and are looking for a new start anyway. We're family and they've always looked up to me. If we can have a nice amount of territory before they get here, by the time they come we're going to be in a position to be filthy rich. How does that sound?"

"Like a fucking plan. So what you wanna do? I'm bout that life. I need that lil cake too." Five gees would fill in the hole that Toya had created with her eviction situation. I didn't like being under ten gees. Five gees was about what you needed in Memphis to make sure that you always had bail money. And a true hustler kept at least twenty gees put up for the retainer of a lawyer. I had to get right, and always keep my daughter up to par. That was my heart.

"Let me get all of my ducks in a row. As soon as I do I'ma call you. I know for sure we gon have to take a trip out to Brooklyn this year. I want you to meet some of the family out there. I got some cousins that's gon eat yo ass alive. Plus, the city is a good time. They do shit way different out there. They helped me to think outside of the box. Life is bigger then Memphis. We gotta get our chips all the way up so we can see that."

I agreed.

***

That night when I made it back to Orange Mound it was two in the morning and Toya was no where to be found. Her car that had at once been parked in front of the crib was no longer there. When I got inside of my place, I found Kamya sitting on the couch reading a book on her tablet. All the lights were off inside of the house except for the one in the kitchen. She looked up at me and smiled then rushed over and wrapped her arms around my neck. "Dang you done had me in this house waiting for you all night. I thought something happened. I was worried out of my mind." She stood on her tippy toes and kissed me in the lips. Traced both with her tongue, then sucked my bottom one into her mouth.

I slid my hands down her back and cuffed her ass. She wore a pair of tight booty shorts. The bottom portions of her ass was fully exposed. Her cheeks were fluffy, and hot. She was born and raised in Memphis. That meant she had that real freaky forbidden shit in her real tough. She, like most of my cousins in Memphis didn't understand what boundaries were. They would be quick to give me   some pussy, and then would have no problem going to lay up with their niggas like nothin ever happened. I wasn't in Memphis long before I started to adopt their ways of doing things. To make matters worst they were all so fuckin bad.

She moaned into my mouth and slid her hand in between us. Kamya gripped my dick and squeezed it, looking up at me with her light brown eyes. "Toya left like two hours ago. I don't know where she went but she said she'll be back in the morning. Shantê's in the room sleeping. She was up all day and night playing that Fortnite and worried about you. The house is quiet, so I'm saying. You gon finally let me get some of this or what?" She unbuttoned and

Ghost

unzipped my pants. Kamya stuck her hand inside of it until she was gripping hot skin.

That codeine started really taking effect. My dick got super hard, real fast. It began to throb in her hand. She rubbed all over the head with her thumb. It caused me to shudder. I kissed her yellow neck and scraped it with my teeth. "You wanna give me some of this young pussy don't you lil cuz."

She stroked my dick. "Hell yeah. I know you fucked Sabrina. I heard y'all. You said that when I turn eighteen that I can get some too. You gotta fuck me now. I'm ready." She moaned, as I slid my hand into her panties from the back. That ass felt hot and soft. I traveled south until I was in her box. Her pussy lips had slight traces of hair all over them as if she'd shaved and now, they were trying to grow back. She licked my neck. "I'm grown now cuz, come on. Fuck me like you're supposed to. I ain't gon tell nobody shit, I swear.

Some how, some way, I found myself seated on the couch with her between my legs. She took my chocolate dick in her hand and stroked it up and down, looking it over. "Damn this is a lot. I see why my sister was scream-ing like you was killing her. I ain't heard Sabrina holler like that since then." Kamya kissed the head and licked all around it. "I'm finna make you fuck me, watch." She pulled her bra under her titties, exposing them. Both golden nip-ples were erect. They looked like pacifiers. She sucked my piece into her mouth and went to work with her lips suck-ing hard.

I threw my head back and groaned in delight. I Gazed down at her and saw her curly hair all over the place. She looked like a sexual goddess. The slurping noises were driving me crazy. I jumped from the couch to slide further down her throat.

"Mmm. Mmm." She popped my dick out. "You gon fuck me cuz, huh? I just wanna feel you in my pussy already. Please." She stroked me faster and faster. Moaning, then she was sucking me all over again like a vet.

I scooted and laid all the way back on the couch. She climbed on top of me with her big ass facing toward me. Her booty shorts were all in her gap, molded to her cleft. I could see the split that separated her pussy lips. Directly in the center of them was a wet spot.

She popped my dick back out. "You ready to fuck me yet cuz. Please?"

Ghost

Chapter 5

I pulled her down so that her panty covered pussy was on my lips. I tried to suck her juices through the thin material. I trapped one of her sex lips and sucked it hard. Her scent was heavy. She smelled like perfume and horney pussy.

"Please fuck me cuz. My pussy throbbing. I know I look way better than Sabrina. Damn I'm so ready." She leaned back down and got to sucking me at full speed. Slurping, and pumping her little fist.

My toes curled up. I pulled her panties to the side and licked up and down her hot slit. Her juices leaked out of her onto my cheek. I sat her cat right in my mouth and sucked it.

She arched her back. "Uhhhhh! Shit. Cuz. Mmm." She continued to jack my dick. "I want you to put this in me so bad. I ain't fucking nobody else until you hit this shit first. Please." Her mouth covered me again. Now she was sucking me like a champion.

"I'ma tear this shit up Kamya. You don't know what you asking for. You just a lil gurl, shawty. You ain't ready for this shit." I opened her lips and licked up and down her groove. I sucked in her clit, holding her pussy to my mouth by gripping her fat ass.

She arched her back again. "Uh. Uh. Uh. Cuz. Please. Uhhh, shit! What's that?" She moaned, before riding my face.

My dick throbbed like crazy. I spread her lips as far as they could go and introduced her to how a grown nigga that loved to eat pussy, ate pussy. My tongue ran circles around her pearl. Then I started flicking it and sucking it into my mouth. She rode my face faster and faster. Her juices poured down my neck. The couch was rocking, telling against the wall. Kamya started to moan louder and louder. She rode me faster. Her titties jiggled. She threw her head back and came with a piercing scream. "Awwww fuck! Awwww. Shiiit!"

I trapped her clit and sucked as firmly as I could before she fell off me. She landed on the floor. Her legs wide open, rubbing her box. Her fingers were coated with her juices. She looked so good playing with her self. I had to admit that out of her two sisters she was the coldest and the most strapped, though Sabrina wasn't that far behind.

I stroked my piece. "Come get this dick Kamya. Finish me off like I did you. Earn this pipe. Come on."

Kamya crawled across the carpet on all fours. Her golden ass was in the air with her long, curly hair falling all over her pretty face. The living room smelled like pussy and perfume. It was intoxicating. It was fuel for our forbidden passion. The closer she got, the more I felt that taboo shit flowing through my veins.

Kamya came and took a hold of my dick, stroking it some more. "I just want you to break me in cuz. I'm ready to fuck, but I ain't messing with these niggas in the Mound like that. I don't trust them, plus my daddy will kill my ass if he found out I gave any one of these niggas some play. But I'm on fire down here." She opened the lips and slid her finger deep inside of her box, bent over and sucked me into her mouth, bobbing frantically.

I closed my eyes to enjoy the feel of the forbidden aspect. It felt so good. I rubbed all over her ass cheeks, and spanked them before sliding down to her cleft, playing wit her ripe pussy. It was so wet that two of my fingers slipped into her with ease. I ran them in and out while she moaned around my pole, gagging, and pulling her bead back only to try again. Her small fist pumped me with expertise.

My eyes rolled into the back of my head. I got to imagining what it would feel like to fuck her from the back. Imagining beating that lil tight pussy in, before I could hold back, I came spurt after spurt straight into her mouth. To my surprise she kept right on sucking, swallowing everything I had to offer.

Cuz popped me out and continued to stroke me. "You ready to fuck this fresh pussy cuz? Tell me you are. You know ain't none if these bitches go shit on me. Look at it." She opened her legs wide and played with her pussy some more.

Man, as much as I was trying to hold back from fucking her, I'd reached my wit's ends. I had to have that ass. I pulled her to me and laid her on the carpet then got in between her thighs. I rubbed my dick up and down her crease, then peeled the fat lips back. Juices oozed out of her hole and ran down into her ass crack. I smeared the big head all around in 'em. Kamya shivered and opened her legs wider. "You sho you want me to fuck this pussy lil one? You sho you ready to take all this?" I slid up and down in between her pussy lips. She got wetter and wetter and wetter. The nipples on her breasts stood up from the mounds a full inch. I licked her neck again.

She tried to reach between her legs, but our bodies prevented her. "I'm ready cuz. I swear to God I'm ready. I want you to fuck me right now." She tried to fit her hand in between us once again. Her thighs opened so wide that I could have sworn I heard a bone pop.

I fit the head right on her hole and started to work myself into her. She closed her eyes and started breathing heavy. Her mouth was wide open. Her pussy was tighter than a fist, despite her wetness.

"Just slam it home cuz. I can take it. I promise I can take it." She rubbed all over my chest to encourage me.

Bomp. Bomp. Bomp. Bomp. Came a knocking on the door. "Phoenix. Phoenix. Boy you bet not be sleep." Toya yelled.

Both me and Kamya scrambled to get our clothes on. I grabbed the Febreze and sprayed to rid the living room from the scent of pussy. "Kamya, go get in my bed wit Shantê. I'ma holler at her and get rid of her ass. I'm bout to fuck that pussy tonight, I ain't trying to hear shit." I could still taste her on my tongue. That was frustrating to me because when I wanted to fuck, I wanted to fuck, and Kamya had me heated. I'd never looked at her in a sexual light until this day.

Kamya nodded and rushed to me and kissed my lips. She rushed down the hallway pulling her shorts out of her juicy yellow ass. She opened the door to my bedroom and closed it softly.

I sprayed some more of the Febreze, then pulled open the door. Toya staggered in smelling like heavy liquor. She crashed into the wall and fell to her knees and got back up laughing. A bottle of Patron was in her right hand. "Boy, I'm fucked up." Toya walked drunkenly to the couch and sat down before she sipped out of the bottle.

I stepped outside and looked both ways. I noticed that Toya's car was parked crooked. Her driver's door was wide opened. The car still running. I jogged outside and turned it off, took the keys out of the ignition, and locked the doors. When I got back inside, she was bent over the garbage can in the kitchen throwing up.

She sat back on her haunches and wiped her mouth. Took another swallow from the bottle. "These niggas so trifling out here Phoenix. They don't got no respect for women. All they care about is themselves." More drinking from the bottle.

I locked my front door and dropped her keys on the table. "Shawty what the fuck is wrong wit you?"

She was quiet for a second. "You, and every nigga that's just like you. I'm so tired of you men treating us like shit. Y'all think y'all can treat us any fuckin way and it's okay. Tell me I'm too dark for any man to ever take me seriously. That I should be lucky anybody a wanna fuck with somebody as burnt as me and you know what'? I believe it." She drank some more of the liquor and stood up. Tears fell down her cheeks.

"Toya what's good wit you? Baby you already know you crushing hoes. You're beautiful. Stop talking this bullshit before my daughter hear it."

She scoffed. "That's all you care about is Shantê ain't it?" More drinking from the bottle. "I stayed in labor for twenty-one hours wit that lil gurl. Damn near lost my life, and all you care about is her. Me and you ain't been right ever since I popped her out and I swear I think it's because you looked down in that delivery room after I told you not to. We ain't been right since." She staggered to the living room. "That a make a woman hate you Phoenix. You make her go through a whole pregnancy. Treat her like a Queen the whole way. She give you a healthy baby's and as soon as it's born you kick the mother to the curb and go find another bitch. All the while you treat that baby like a God. That a make then mother hate you Phoenix. So many men do that to us women and I swear to God it'll make us hate you!" Toya threw the bottle to the carpet. It bounced and rolled across it, spilling its contents along the way.

I jumped back. "Toya, I ain't never kicked you to the curb. I still care about you. That'll never change." That liquor must have been affecting her in a crazy way. I'd never seen her act like this before.

"That's bullshit Phoenix, and you know it. Let me ask you something. How do you think Mikey would feel if he found out that you and Alicia been fucking around behind his back, huh?"

A chill ran down my spine. "Fuck is you talking about?" I played dumb.

She waved me off. "Nigga I know y'all been fuckin since high school. I done caught y'all a few times, watched, shaking my head and didn't say nothing. Then any fool can tell when y'all are in the same room. That girl can't keep her eyes off you. Every time I saw that shit it pissed me off, but I didn't care you know why?"

"I still don't know what the fuck you talking about but humor me."

"Because I had Bryon. Bryon loved me. He was the only man that seemed to appreciate my dark skin. He made me feel beautiful. Told me that I was a blessing straight from the motherland. Then, the way he made love to me was something amazing. Umph. Lord knows I'ma miss that." She looked up to me and frowned. "But you took him away from me! You killed the only man that ever loved me!" She screamed. "I hate you!" She stood up with both of her fists balled.

I peeked down the hall, expecting both Shantê and Kamya to come running out of the back room. "Yo, shut yo ass up. You always doing too much."

"Nall fuck that! I'm tired of shutting up. You don't care about me. All you care about is that little girl that I gave birth too. If she wasn't apart of the equation you would have quit fucking wit me a long time ago. Why did you kill Bryon!"

This broad was tripping. I didn't know what the fuck was going on with her. She walked into my face with her fist balled. "Man, Toya you better sit yo ass down. I ain't playing wit you right now. Shut yo ass up."

"No! What you gon do? You gon kill me like you did my man, and all for what? Because he whooped her lil ass after she got smart wit him. That's what he should of done. She's only eight. Some man need to whoop her ass because you won't."

Smack. I hit her hard. Imagining a grown as man beating my baby with her mother condoning it was too much for me. "Watch yo muthafuckin mouth. You bet not never condone some nigga hitting my baby. I'm her father. Not nam other muthafucka. You hear me?"

"Fuck you. Fuck you and her. Y'all can have each other. You ain't gon be around for long anyway. When them Black Haven niggas get a hold of yo ass for what you did to Bryon its gon be hell to pay the captain. Mark my words on that. You gon get yours."

Shantê appeared in the hallway with a small blanket wrapped around her shoulders. "Mommy, why are you crying?" She asked, stepping toward her.

Toya snapped. "Bitch I ain't cha mama, he is. He ya mama and ya daddy from here on out. I hate both of you. You ruined my life, and ya daddy. I wish I never had you. I almost lost you in my third month. Man, I wish that would have happened. Every time I look at you all I see is the little girl that ruined my life. Now get!" She stomped her foot at Shantê.

Shantê jumped backwards and fell on her butt. As soon as she fell, she broke into a fit of tears. This pissed me off. Kamya picked her up and began to bounce up and down with her mugging Toya.

"Yellow bitch what the fuck is you looking at? You got something you wanna say? Huh?" Toya cracked her knuckles in a display of aggression.

I pointed down the hallway. "Y'all go in the room. I'm finna deal wit her. I'm sick of this shit." I was warming up like an oven getting ready to cook a pizza. The more I saw the fear on my daughter's face, the angrier I got.

Toya rushed into the hallway, blocking their path. "Aw hell nall. If you gon kill me like you killed Bryon, there is going to be some witnesses this time. Oh, wait I forgot. You dumb ass nigga. Did you know that he had a bitch upstairs when you did what you did? He wasn't the only one home. That bitch saw us get in your truck and drive away, and instead of going to the police she went to his brothers in Black Haven because she got warrants out on her ass. Aw! You better be lucky she did, or your stupid ass a be in jail right now!" She screamed.

My heart dropped into my stomach. I wondered if Toya was making this shit up because she was drunk. I was hoping she was. I knew I couldn't have been that stupid. There had been no signs that anybody else had been there. We'd made a huge commotion, and nobody had said shit. I racked my brain to replay the situation. All the while Toya kept on running her mouth. When I remembered that Bryon had been setting two sets of plates for the food, he'd been cooking I was devastated. Fuck, she was right.

"Get out of our way Toya so we can do what Phoenix said. You stank, and smell like alcohol. Don't nobody wanna smell that." Kamya muttered, mugging her with obvious anger.

"Yeah mama, move. You're making me sad because of what you said. You're nothin but a meanie." Shantê hollered.

"A meanie?" Toya grabbed Shantê by the hair and yanked her to the floor.

Shantê screamed, before the back of her head banged on the floor. But after it hit the linoleum, she really got to hollering as loud as she could.

Then I lost it.

Ghost

Chapter 6

"Get off me Phoenix. Let me go! Let me go! Toya roared beating at by back with her fists. "I hate your guts. You and that lil bitch. I hate y'all guts."

I opened the door to her car and tossed her into the driver's seat. I got into the passenger seat and turned on the ignition. "Drive the fucking car. Back this bitch away from my crib right now. I don't give a fuck how drunk you is, you ain't staying here tonight. Drive!"

"Why I gotta leave huh? Why do you hate me so much? Huh? I won't going no muthafuckin where. I got every right to be in there as them too. You better look at these stretch marks again, there ain't many, but its enough to re-mind yo ass of what I sacrificed for you." She opened the door to the car and ran out into the parking lot, up the short walkway, and to my door. Once there she twisted the knob and ran back inside of the house. She left the door wide open.

My patience was wearing thin. I was minutes away of beating her ass. I was trying yo refrain from doing that as much as I could, but she was making it so hard.

When I got back into the house, her and Kamya were in the living room wrestling, and grunting on the floor. Toya straddled Kamya trying to slap her face over and over. "Bitch, you better watch yo mouth. I'll kill you. I'll kill yo lil yellow ass. Kill you just like he did my man!" Toya swore.

"Get off me. Get off me you crazy ass Bitch. What the fuck is your problem?" Kamya asked trying to pump her hips to get Toya up off her with little success.

"Stop mommy. Stop. What's wrong with you? Get off my cousin. You're acting stupid." Shantê cried. Her little face was red, and wet with tears.

I'd had enough. I grabbed a hand full of Toya's hair and pulled her off Kamya. "Shantê, and Kamya, go into my bedroom and lock the door. Hurry up. Now." I growled with Toya smacking at my hands.

They ran down the hall and did as they were told. Shantê continued crying along the way. I could hear Kamya trying to calm her down once they were on the other side of the door.

Toya mule kicked me in the nuts, dropping me. I fell to one knee and had to gather myself. It felt like I was getting ready to throw up. I was out of breath and everything. My hand stole to my crotch to try and ease the pain, but it only made things worse. "I'm finna kick yo ass, Toya." In that moment the threat was idle. She could of did whatever she wanted to do to me at that time and I wouldn't have been able to do anything.

She ran a few feet and turned around to face me. "I hate you Phoenix. You ruined my life. You took the only man away from me that could have loved me. I'll never forgive you for that. I swear to God you gon reap what you've sown." She opened the door to the house and ran out of it, after snatching her car keys from the table. If I would of had any strength in me at that time I would of chased after her and probably did some things that I would have regretted. A minute later I heard her car start. Then there was the sound of the wheels burning rubber as she backed out of the parking space and peeled away from my place.

***

The next morning, I woke up to Mikey beating on the door. I had been so mad the night prior that I'd fallen asleep on the couch in the living room. Somewhere in the middle of the night, Kamya had come and tried to wake me up so we could talk, but I was so heated that I ordered her to go back into the room with Shantê because I needed to think. Well thinking turned into me falling asleep, and I was awakened out of my sleep the first thing in the morning by Mikey.

I pulled open the door, and he walked right past me. "Mane, yo baby mama crazy as hell lil one. Brought her ass over my crib last night drunk as a skunk. Arguing wit Alicia about ruining her life. Didn't say how she ruined it, only that she did." He shook his head. He was puffing on a fat ass blunt. A thick gray smoke rose from its tip and descended from his nostrils as he exhaled.

I ran my hand over my waves. "Shawty was over here on that fuck shit too. She starting to have remorse over Bryon's death. You know how that shit go. I guess that fool must have been pumping her head up wit a bunch of bullshit. Now she feeling like he was the only one that could ever love her. It's bananas. Let me hit that sauce."

He handed me the blunt. "I'm over here bright and early because we about to go peel somebody head back for my connect. This gon be the first move that's gon catapult us to where we need to be. I need you to get dressed, and bring that forty-five I gave you, just in case." He walked into the kitchen and opened my refrigerator and pulled out a carton of orange juice. "You want me to whip up some breakfast real quick?"

I yawned and stretched my arms over my head. I was sleepy as hell. The bud tasted good though. It was harsh to the chest, but it got me high right away. In a matter of

57

minutes, I looked Asian. "You even know who we about to holler at, or is this a blind mission?"

"Oh, I know Potna. When you ever known me to jump into some shit head first without knowing what the deal was. Think about it homeboy." He pointed to his temple and took a swallow of the orange juice.

I had to piss worse than a little kid scared to get up at night and go and use the bathroom. "Well I need to know what's good. Also, if we about to hit this lick, what are the residuals?"

Mikey sat the juice on the table in the kitchen and went into his pocket. He started to count a knot of hundreds. "Here go five bands right here. That's what I promised you for this first move. This is five, and the second move gone bring you ten, and so forth and so on. Keep in mind that everything I'm making that I'm busting down the middle with you because that's how its supposed to be. Now hurry up and get dressed Mane. I know you can use that green."

"Hell yeah, I can. Make some eggs nigga. I need to put a sandwich on my stomach or something."

"I got you, just hurry up Potna. Time is money." He pulled the carton of eggs out of the refrigerator and opened the cabinet.

I made my way down the hallway. Just before I got to the bathroom Kamya opened the bedroom door and rushed into the bathroom. Before she could close it, I stuck my foot in the crack of the door. "Hold on lil cuz. I gotta piss like a muthafucka."

"Me too. You better come in, but I'm going first." She pulled up the toilet seat and sat down on. Seconds later I heard her tinkling into the water. That only made me have to piss even worse.

I stood there shifting my weight from one foot to the other. As soon as she hopped up, I flushed the toilet, then I started to go. It felt so good that I closed my eyes and moaned a lil bit. That morning piss was everything. After I finished, I washed my hands.

Kamya stepped on the side of me and kissed my neck and licked up and down the thick vein on the side of it. "I don't know what her problem was last night, but I hate that she messed up what we had going on. I wanted some of this." She whispered. She snuck her hand inside my boxers and squeezed my dick then made eye contact with me in the mirror.

"Don't even trip, we gon get a chance to do our thing. You can bank on that." I turned to face Kamya, pulled her to me and gripped that fat ass. Giving her a wedgie. She moaned and threw her head back. I sucked all over her neck. Slipped my fingers into her shorts, and then into her gap once again from the back. She opened her legs. I was Eager to finger her at full speed. It was early in the morning and her pussy was wetter than soup. I hugged her body to mine. "Cum in these fingers lil cuz. Make that kitty swallow these digits."

She breathed hard. Her mouth wide open, slamming back on the two fingers that were working in and out of her. "Stop. Stop Phoenix. Uh, stop." She gripped my dick and tried to stroke it while I fingered her. "Uhhh shit." Her scent rose into the air.

Faster and faster my fingers went. In and out. Over and over. Then I was playing with her erect clitoris, rubbing it in circles. Then got her to going crazy. I made her bend over the tub. Once she bent over, I got to fingering that pussy hard, and swift. I watched how the lips opened and swallowed my fingers. They were wet and slimy in a matter of minutes. I rubbed all over her moon and made her cum screaming into the drying towel. Her knees buckled. When she got to reaching for the button to my pants, I knocked her hand away. Mikey began to call me from the kitchen. I sucked my fingers into my mouth, loving the taste of her juices. "We gon handle this bidness tonight lil cuz. You hear me?"

She slid her hand into her panties and nodded. "We better. I'm tired of playin games wit you. You better give me some. Oh, and I got somethin for you that I ain't been able to give you yet. You want me to go get it right now?" She asked, standing up.

"Nall. I'll get it when I get home later. I need you to watch Shantê. I should be back in a few hours. Mikey want me to handle some bidness wit him real quick."

"But you know I gotta be to work by nine o'clock. Do you think you'll be back before then?" She flipped her long hair behind her shoulders.

"I hope so. I mean I don't know for sure, but if I ain't I'll just pay you for the hours you missed. How does that sound?"

She shrugged her shoulders. "Its ain't even about that. You know I work wit them old folks and thangs. My company be wanting us to give them a forty eight hour notice when we set to call off. I mean I could just bring Shantê along with me. My client is cool, she shouldn't say nothing."

I nodded. "Well either way, you do what you gotta do. I'll still hit you and make sure that you're good. Toya being stupid right now. I don't know when she gon snap out of that dumb shit. But I appreciate you though."

She smiled. "Well you already know how you can show me your gratitude. My lil kitty thirsty right now. I want some of this." She cupped my dick again, then kissed my lips. Sucking on them hard, moaning.

I cuffed that ass again. She was so thick. I yanked her shorts upward, so that her cheeks were exposed. "Tonight baby. Tonight, I'ma wear this ass out. That's my word."

Bomp. Bomp. Bomp. "Nigga come on. What the hell you in there doing? You got diarrhea or somethin."

Kamya broke her kiss and stepped back. "It better be tonight. I'm serious, too." She kissed me again, broke it, and unlocked the door. She stepped into the hallway with her shorts all up in her ass.

Mikey was standing in front of the door. When he saw her, he had to step back. He watched her walk down the hallway and into my bedroom. When she disappeared, he shook his head. "Dawg she eighteen now right?"

I laughed and nodded. "Yeah why you ask that?"

"Man, she so cold now bruh. On everythang. I never thought she would get that thick. You remember how skinny she used to be?" He made a sour face. "Now lil one got mo ass den a horse. It's fucked up I'm married. I should have waited for lil mama. I bet she got that sauce too. Damn." He laughed and signaled me to follow him. "Come on. I hooked you up this cheese omelet. Then we gotta get on bidness."

I didn't know if Kamya had that sauce or not, but I had every intention on finding out this night.

61

Ghost

Chapter 7

"Dis shit plain and simple Homeboy, my connect want this building and the one right next to it. That mean that you and yo niggas gotta get the fuck out of here, and I'm talking like right now or else it's gon be a problem." Mikey said, staring the dark-skinned man in the eye as he sat across the long table from him.

We were at a catfish warehouse on the east side of Memphis. It smelled so bad in there that I felt sick on the stomach. Behind the dark-skinned man were two other big dark-skinned dudes with smirks on their faces, and their arms crossed in front of their chests. They must have thought it was sweet. I was glad they did because as long as they kept their arms crossed in front of them that meant that I would be able to get to my pistol before they could get to theirs. Me and Mikey had visions of starting our own cartel, and whoever this plug was, he made it seem like they could help us to get established. I was all in like poker chips, and ready for action.

The heavy set, dark skinned man, had long dreads, and red eyes. He smoked on a hefty blunt that smelled like it was mixed with cocaine. He blew the smoke in Mikey's face. "You tell your connect that I said to kiss my ass. That I aint going no fuckin where and neither is my niggas. We run this shit now. Its time Memphis gets a makeover." He took a strong pull from his blunt and inhaled.

Mikey clenched his jaw. His hand slipped under the table. "Look bruh, I don't know where the fuck you came from, but I assure you that it is in your best interest to move around. The cards ain't in your favor Potna. We gon need that territory, and this warehouse for bigger and better thangs. This your last warning. You gon take heed, or you gon be hard headed? Pick your path Potna. What's it gon be?"

The fat man broke into a fit of laughter. He scooted his chair back from the table, cracking up. "You hear this brown son of a bitch. He in my shit talking like he the toughest muthafucka on this side of the Dixie. I ain't never seen nothin like this. You gotta be high off that Rebirth heroin that everybody getting wind of."

I continued to size up his men. The fact that they'd allowed for us to come into their presence without being patted down told me that they were rookies to the game. I don't know if they underestimated Memphis niggas or what. Maybe they thought we were soft or not about that life, but whatever it was I was about to take pride in whatever was about to go down.

"Check this out tough guy. You tell your connect, whoever they are, that there is a new sheriff in town, and he ain't going no where. Tell them that I am a war that they don't want to start. You got all of that?"

Mikey nodded his head. "Aw yeah muthafucka. I got all of that. Now you take all of this." He rose from his seat with two forty fives. The red beams appeared on the heavyset man's face, and then he was pulling the triggers. The guns spit rapidly. Bullet after bullet ate away at his face, slowly melting it away. Shells hopped out of the gun and wound up clinking on the table.

His security went to reach for their weapons but before they could uncross their arms, I lit 'em up like Christmas trees. All chest and neck shots. If my nigga was bussing, then I was too. The two goons fell on top of one another. A big pool of blood formed under their bodies.

Mikey pulled a Ziploc bag out of his waist band. Placed both guns on his hip and pulled out a knife. He grabbed the fat man by his dreads and slid him across the floor. My dude reached into his mouth and pulled his tongue out and sawed it off, then dropped it into the Ziploc bag. His eats were next. I didn't know what that was about, and I didn't ask. Memphis was a muthafucka. In order to stay alive, I had to go with the flow until everything flowed directly through me.

Mikey hopped up and looked down at the man. "Punk ass nigga. His history caught up wit 'em homeboy. I'll explain his fuck ways later. Help me wrap these niggas up and get rid of their bodies. We got a lot of chopping up to do so let's get a move on. I gotta get the tools out of my truck." He jogged off.

That morning we wound up cutting up all three of them niggas before dumping they ass in a creek. The only parts of their bodies that were salvaged were the ear lobes and tongue of the chump that was supposed to be calling the shots.

***

"We gotta get this money Phoenix. Its getting hot outside and we gotta get our bands all the way up." Mikey said later that same afternoon. We were in his kitchen at one of his spots in Orange Mound. He took the mayonnaise jar full of liquid coke and swished it around with oven mitts on.

I took the half of brick that had already rocked up and sat at the kitchen table. I had a surgical mask over my face. I didn't like the smell of dope when it was cooking. That shit hurt my head. Plus, I couldn't risk that shit getting into my system. I didn't have no habits other then codeine and pussy, and I wasn't trying to get none. I took my razor blade and got right to work. I was finna bag the entire eighteen zips into dimes, in the end my profit would be a little over fifty gees. In Orange Mound you were able to make twenty-eight hundred off an ounce, so when I multiply that by eighteen, and factored in the shorts I'd take, I was looking at fifty plus bands. That was cool wit me. "Mikey, I'm ready to eat nigga. When we gon meet this plug, you keep talking so much about?" I chopped off about a zip. Pulled the digital scale closer to me and got to doing my thing.

He turned off the fire on the stove and set his Mayonnaise jar in some cool water. He had a light blue doctor's mask over the lower portion of his face as well. "We gon meet the connect at the end of the week. We've got one more move to pull. I ain't even expect this bird we just got. This some extra shit, but I'm thankful for it. We gon have lil Smoke nem push these dimes for us while we handle some other shit. I already know you ain't no trap nigga. Bruh, you still know how to cut hair?"

I was focused. I'd already bagged two zips with lightning speed. That was fifty-six hunnit ready to go. "You can't forget no shit like that, why what's good?" I continued to do my thing. My phone buzzed on my lap. I looked at the picture and saw Toya's picture pop up. The text across the bottom read: Come get me. I'm at my aunty house. I'm sorry." I ignored the message.

"Cause when I open this barber shop, I want you to have a chair. We can't be in these streets forever nigga. We living on borrowed time."

"Nigga never. I'll never work for no nigga. I gotta be my own boss. Until then, I'ma be right here in the slums getting money the hard way. Broke ain't cute. And the workforce ain't for me. I hate authority figures." I bagged another zip with ease and went right into the next one.

"Yeah I hear that. But you be with me. I'm greedy. I gotta have that legal money and that street shit. I also got an end game because I know this thug life shit don't last forever. I'ma pump a few babies into Alicia. By me knowing that I have, to ensure that she and our children won't ever be in need for nothin if somethin should ever happen to me. That mean I gotta be spaced out. Gotta go hard, but that endgame is important. All hustlers must have an end game."

I knew he was speaking that truth. I thought about that every single day, and it was happening more and more the crazier Toya acted. I had to make sure that Shantê was going to be well taken care of. She was my life at this point. I needed to find something I could exit the game into just like Mikey had. It was time that I grew up mentally and got my priorities in line.

My phone buzzed again, another text from Toya. This time she was begging me to come and get her. She even sent the crying emoji. I dusted my hands off and told her to give me two hours, that I was on something. I didn't know what I was going to do for sure, but I didn't feel like being bothered with her. I had plans on taking Kamaya's ass down tonight. I couldn't have her cock blocking. "Say Mikey, I don't know what my end game is yet, but I'ma find one. I know that's important."

As soon as I finished those words, Smoke knocked on the door. Mikey let him in, he had two of his lil guys with him. Smoke was dark skinned. Skinny, with short dreads and gold teeth that his brother had copped for him before he went to the Feds. He was born and bred in Orange Mound.

He saw me and walked right over. "Aw hell nall. What up Playboy? Yo name ringing like a muthafucka."

I was on my seventh zip. Focused. "What you talking about Smoke?" I didn't even look up at him. I wanted to get my shit bagged up so I could count my profits. I needed this fifty gees. I had to take Shantê shopping soon. She was growing out of everything.

"Mane, they say you suckered that Bryon nigga out of Black Haven. The whole Mound talking about that shit. They say you beat that nigga senseless in front of his pregnant baby mother. Then told her that she bet not say shit. That bitch was so spooked that she ran all the way back to Jackson, Mississippi. Yousa savage." He laughed and rested his hand on my shoulder.

I looked at his hands and then up to him. He removed it quick. "Lil Homie you can't believe everything you hear. I ain't have no beef wit that man. This the first time I'm hearing about somebody bodying his ass. That's fucked up." I fronted and kept right on bagging my work. I was thinking fuck Bryon. I did wonder how word had managed to travel so quickly to and through the Mound though. But that was classic Memphis. Word spread faster than a person scratching a rash in this city.

Smoke smacked his lips. "Man, aiight. Well it ain't for you to confirm or deny it. I'm just saying the streets talk, Durty. And they saying that you're a beast. I honor that big homie."

Mikey stepped into the living room. "Mane what the fuck I tell yo lil ass about all dat gossip shit?" He snapped.

"Bruh I was just letting playboy know what it is. Dat way he a know why everybody looking at him all crazy and shit. What, I shouldn't have said anything?"

Mikey scoffed. "You just sit yo lil ass down and bag his dope. You and yo homeboys. Y'all worried about the wrong thangs. Sides, Phoenix couldn't have stanked that Black Haven nigga cuz bruh was wit me at the funeral home helping David all day and night the same time they saying that shit happened." He sat about nine zips on the table and three razor blades.

"Oh, so you did hear about it then?" Smoke asked placing his North Face jacket on the back of his chair. Why he had a jacket on when it was hot as hell outside was beyond me. Though it did look as if it was going to rain within the next hour or so.

"Yeah, I heard that rumor, but that shit ain't true. Now shut the fuck up and grab a blade. I want all dimes. Make likes of twenty-eight hunnit like bruh doing. Phoenix let me holler at you over here for a minute Mane."

I as on my eleventh zip, bagging away. I hated to stop but I had to see what the homie wanted. He looked a lil thrown off, like something was wrong. So, we met up in the back room.

"Bruh, I forgot to tell you about that shit. You know they say that Toya went to Eighteen Forty Tavern around the corner and got to blabbing her mouth on some drunk shit saying that you bodied dude ass?"

I shook my head. "Hell nall. When was this?"

"Last night. Say she was crying and everything. Talking about first you killed her nigga, and then you kicked her out into the cold. Bruh we gotta put a cork in her bottle before you wind up in a sticky position. We also gotta holler at dude's baby mother in Jackson. If they the only two that can put that shit on you, we need to do something about it. I'm serious. I ain't trying to lose you bruh. You my nigga. What you wanna do?"

Man, I was dumbfounded. I couldn't believe that Toya would pop off like that in front of strangers. Family was one thing, but strangers was another. She was putting me out there bad. I was so confused that I didn't know what to do. I knew I was finna hit the Jackson bitch though.

Pregnant or not. Fuck that. "Man Mikey, what do you think I should do?" I was lost.

He placed his hand on my shoulder. "To be honest wit you." He took a deep breath and sighed. "Man, you might have to be a single parent. She playin wit yo life, bruh. You already know they don't play no games in Tennessee when it comes to what she trying to get pinned on you. Its either you make her put a pin in this bull shit she's spreading, or you gon have to send her to the same place that fool Bryon is. Its that simple. Right now, she acting real crazy. Talking about how much she hate your daughter and shit. Bruh, it's real bad. You ain't got no other choice other than to handle that situation, it's getting out of hand."

Damn. I felt like I had the stomach flu. I couldn't believe it had come down to something like this. I didn't know why Toya was acting so fucking stupid. Why she was saying the things that she was but clearly, she was trying to either start an uprising, or get me popped. The way she was talking about Shantê I wondered what her game plan was with my baby? If she got me popped, or smoked, what would she do with our baby? That question spooked me more then anything else.

Mikey stood in silence watching me. "Mane I don't know what's going through yo brain right now, but whatever it is I'm riding wit you to the fullest. I'd hate to send Toya on her way, so you'd have to do all of that, but you already know I won't have no problem sending her ass into the oven. I fucks wit you the long way bruh, and I love Shantê like that my lil shawty fa real. Her mama off her rocker right now. You gotta crush that beast that she's trying to build. You feel me?"

"Yeah I feel you Playboy. I'ma text her ass right now and see if there is somewhere that we can meet up. Shawty

70

on one right now, and I can't have her do me in like that."
I sent Toya a quick text at the same time I was telling
Mikey this. Told her that we need to holler. I was coming
to pick her up ASAP.

"Yeah bruh, we got big thangs about to take place in
our future. We can't let shawty ruin that shit all because
she was head over heels for that fuck nigga who put his
hands on my God daughter. That ain't how that work. Just
remember that I'm riding with you in whatever you decide.
Its love Potna. Til the dirt." He hugged me and stepped out
of the room.

I stayed in there for a few more minutes trying to gather
my thoughts. I waited for Toya to text me back. When she
finally agreed for me to come and pick her up from her
Auntie's house, I responded that I was on my way. I finally
stepped back into the living room and set four zips in front
of Smoke. "Huh lil nigga. You pop three of these for me
and the fourth one is all you. I need you to stay on your
bidness lil homie. We trying to put these chips together for
something greater. We got you lil niggas in mind. Don't
trip."

Smoke smiled. "Mane, you niggas eating like a mafucka homeboy. I don't know what y'all up too, but long
as y'all got me and my potnas in mind when you get to it,
then its all gravy wit me, Durty. I got this work for you.
Give me four days."

Ghost

Chapter 8

When I left Mikey's trap, I went all the way over to Toya's Aunty's house just as it was starting to storm outside. When I pulled up on State street, she was just bending the corner. Toya pulled up behind my truck and jumped out of her car with her jacket over her head. She knocked on the window, until I popped the lock, then she got in. Lightning flashed across the sky. The rain was coming down in a steady pitter patter on top of the roof of my truck. "Damn, its raining bad as hell out there baby. And it seems like it just came out of nowhere." She said this and slammed the door.

I turned the heat up a lil more. She'd let in a draft. I smelled her perfume and the scent pissed me off. I started remembering everything that Mikey had said, and it only added to my anger. I pulled away from the curb with thoughts of rolling a few blocks so we could holler.

"Baby why are you so quiet?" She asked reaching over and squeezing my thigh.

I flicked her hand off me. "Don't touch me, shawty. What the fuck is your problem, Toya?"

"Aw shit. Here we go wit dis bullshit. Nigga I know you ain't bring yo ass all the way over here just so you can get on some dumb shit? Ain't nobody got time for none of that shit. You can drop me back off." She started to texting on her phone.

I felt myself getting heated already. For some reason whenever I was in her presence lately it was a common feeling. I started to wonder if I'd ever felt anything for her. "Shawty why you going around running yo mouth in some got damn Tavern about what happened wit Bryon? You trying to get a nigga locked up or stanked out here in these streets?" I asked, mugging her.

"Nigga I ain't trying to do shit. You shoulda never killed my nigga. You brought this shit on yo self. And I don't remember saying nothing to nobody. I must if need faded a something. Drop me back off. I don't wanna hear this shit." She crossed her arms and looked straight ahead as if she were set on having an attitude.

"Toya, on everythang, Mane I'm tryin as hard as I can to not fuck you up right now. You been on some dumb shit for the last week. Saying that stupid shit to our baby. Popping off about dude situation and attacking my lil cousin and shit. Bitch, you know if you was anybody else that I would have gotten up wit yo glamour already, especially when it comes to that rat shit."

"Phoenix, I ain't worried about you doing nothing to me. I ain't scared of you. You ain't nothin but another one of these niggas in Memphis to me. Whatever you gon do, you gon do anyways. Nigga I ain't worried. Far as I'm concerned, Mane, fuck you." She said this without even looking over at me.

I was so heated that I was shaking. I looked her over and curled my top lip. "Toya, if you ain't have my daughter I woulda smoked yo ass already. You out playin right now, when life ain't a game. You risking my life. Making it seem like you don't care about Shanté's. I'm wondering why I'm even giving you a pass right now." Achill went down my spine. I was shaking so bad that I knew I was on the verge of snapping. I could see Toya's corpse in my head, and I ain't feel no remorse about that. I pulled up to Widow's Peak, a spot that over looked the city and parked my truck. I reached down and took the forty-five from under my seat and set it on my lap. The rain seemed to fall harder against my windshield. The wipers swished back and forth loudly.

Toya looked over at the gun and sighed. "So that's why you brought me out here huh, Phoenix? You brought me out so you can kill me?" She scrunched up her face, blinked, and allowed tears to roll down her cheeks.

I cocked my banger. My heart was getting heavy. I didn't want to do what I knew I had to, but Toya was leaving me with no choice. "Toya, I don't wanna do this to yo ass but you playin a dirty game, shawty. I can't have you putting me and my daughter's life at risk all because you feeling some type of way over that Bryon nigga. You gon either get yo shit together, or I'ma have to handle you just like I would one of these niggas on the street. You ain't giving me much of a choice."

She was quiet for a moment. The wind blew harshly and caused the truck to sway from side to side. The pitter patter of the rainfall grew louder, then lightning flashed across the sky, before the thunder roared angrily. "You know what Phoenix. Yousa bitch ass nigga. If you think I'm about to cower to you, or beg you to not kill me, you got the game fucked up. Like I said before, I ain't scared of you, homeboy. Ever since I had that lil girl you been treating me real foul, as if you had an agenda all along. Don't nobody love me Phoenix. After I gave us a child, the one place I should of been able to look for love was to you. But that's when the bitches and hoes started to fly from your mouth. That's when you started to fuck wit a bunch of females and push me to the side. Unbeknownst to you I was dealing with postpartum depression like crazy. Cutting on my wrists and shit. Boy, I ain't know if I wanted to live or die. During that whole process all you did was treat me like shit. So, you know what, pull that trigger nigga, because if you don't, I don't know what I'ma do to you, or have done. I hate your fucking guts. Yousa bitch to me." Toya sucked her teeth. "Yeah."

I clenched my jaw muscles over and over. My heart was beating faster than I could ever remember. My vision started to go hazy. I was getting madder by the second. I didn't know what to say to her. What to think? What to feel? I just wanted to react. Be impulsive.

"Well, what you waiting on Phoenix? I ain't never known you to be scared to pop that pistol. Nigga I'm ready to go right now. Kill me. Kill me, or I swear to God if you don't its gon be the biggest mistake you ever made."

I snapped and aimed the gun at her. She froze. "Toya. Bitch I'm tired of you running your mouth. You think shit is a game when it ain't. Now I don't know what the fuck you smoking, but you seconds away from losing your life. The only thing stopping me right now is a Shantê. You're her mother. I won't be able to look my baby in the eyes for the rest of her life."

A pair of bright headlights that flashed into my truck. Then a van rolled along side of us and parked. A smile came across Toya's face. "Lucky for me I don't give a fuck what Shantê think. I wanna see you explain yourself to Bryon's brothers about what you did to him."

I looked past her shoulder and saw three dark figures appear on the side of the van. Somebody started knocking on her passenger's window so hard that I was worried about them breaking the glass.

I lowered the gun. "Who the fuck is that?"

"I told you that shit wasn't over." She opened the door to the truck and dropped to the ground, and then the shooting started.

Boom. Boom. Boom. Boom.

The window shattered on my truck. The body rocked from side to side. Big holes formed in the door. I didn't waste time, I started bussing back to back at the figures. *Boom. Boom. Boom. Boom.* Without missing a beat, I threw the truck in reverse and backed out.

They fired more shots. *Boom. Boom. Boom. Boom.* My windshield shattered into my lap leaving it filled with glass. I ducked down and fired five more shots before I threw the truck in drive and stormed away from the scene. I took one final glance into the rearview mirror to see what I could see. Seconds later the back window shattered. All I saw was three big niggas with guns in their hands running back to their van. Once there they threw Toya in the side door and slammed it back.

"I'ma kill that Bitch!" I snapped, storming away.

***

Fearing the worst, I sped back to my crib in Orange Mound, and woke my daughter and Kamya up. "Get up y'all. Get up now!" I shook the bed to help them awake. I knew that it was only a matter of time before Toya told Bryon's brothers where we laid our heads. I was convinced that she'd texted them niggas our location in the hopes that they would kill me. Since I knew that was the case, when I caught her ass it was over for her.

Shantê woke up whining. "I don't feel like waking up daddy. I'm sleepy. I'm just a kid."

Kamya, wiped her mouth. "Phoenix, what's the matter? You seemed frazzled?"

"Kamya, y'all gotta get up. Toya on some more bullshit. I gotta make sure that y'all are safe. Shantê get yo ass up." I tapped her on the butt.

She jumped out of the bed hollering. "Okay daddy. Okay." She slid her pants up her night gown and fastened them. She put her Jordans on her little feet.

Across the way Kamya got dressed as well. We were rushing out of my apartment in Orange Mound, and to my truck.

The rain had let up. It slowed to a drizzle. When Kamya saw my truck, she stopped in her tracks. "What the hell happened to that? She asked pointing at it.

"Don't worry about it. Come on, let's jump in your whip." And that's just what we did.

I got into the back seat and laid down with my book bag full of dope and money. I was so angry that it had brought on a pounding migraine. I was gon get them niggas and Toya too.

As we were rolling out of the parking lot to Orange Mound, the same van from earlier was pulling into it. They drove past us and stormed into the lot toward my place. I sat up and watched them park in front of my truck. Then Kamya turned down the avenue and I could no longer see them. Multiple shots sounded before we completely pulled away from the area. That told me everything that I needed to know. Bryon's people were going to be a problem.

"I don't know what's going on Phoenix, but I think we should stay at my place until you figure thangs out. From the way yo truck looked cuz, somebody is trying to take you out the game Mane. You might as well lay low for a lil while."

I sighed. "Who all over here, Kamya?"

"Nobody. I don't be having folks all up in my crib and thangs. I've only had it for a few months. I mean my daddy come through every now and then, but he don't stay there. Its just gon be us. And at least Toya don't know where I stay. That gotta be a plus." She met my eyes in her rearview mirror. "Plus, we got unfinished bidness anyway Durty." She smiled at that.

"Daddy, what my mama do? Is she mad at us?" Shanté asked, turning around in her seat.

I kissed her forehead. "Yo mama wiling right now. She'll get it together soon. Until she do you gon stay close to cousin Kamya. If your phone ring and its your mother whatever you do, do not tell her where you are, or who you're with until we figure something's out. Do you understand me baby girl?"

She nodded. "Yes daddy, but I'm scared because of those gun shots in your truck. My mama hates me and if somebody shoot you then I'm not gon have nobody. That's not fair." She turned back around and crossed her arms in front of her chest like Toya had a habit of doing.

"Shanté, ain't nobody about to shoot your father. You need to stop saying that. Its not good to wish bad luck on people." Kamya chastised her.

"Its not good for you to think you my mama either and try to tell me what to do. You ain't that much older than me, so mind yo bidness. Umph." She rolled her eyes and started to play on her tablet.

Kamya shook her head and we locked eyes once again in the rearview mirror. "This lil girl is too much at times Phoenix. I swear her mouth is too sharp. She must get that from Toya."

I didn't have a response. My brain was spinning like a top. I had to get a hold of this Bryon situation and fast. I didn't know who his brothers were, but I would have to do my research. If them niggas was coming at me like that, they had to be some major niggas. I also wondered where Toya fit in with them? Were they going to dump her body after using her to track me down? Or had she officially crossed over to them and was something like their Queen of whatever they had going? I didn't know, but I couldn't stop my brain from racing like a NASCAR driver. I didn't like for nobody to have me on the fence. Especially niggas that I didn't even know. The worst enemy a man could have was the kind of enemy that he didn't know. I feared these niggas not because of what they could do to me, but because I didn't know how they moved. I didn't know how to attack back, because I didn't know where they were from.

"Phoenix, I just want you to know that I got your back cuz. Just lean back for a few days wit me. Gather your thoughts, and then you'll know how to handle your bidness. I love you too." She smiled.

I was so angry that I didn't even return her I love you. I wanted to kill something. That was the only emotion that I wanted to explore.

Chapter 9

I wound up laying low for a full week, and the only reason I did was because the same night that I'd gotten into the shoot out with Bryon' people I didn't know two things. The first was that I'd hit one of them three times in the chest and he was in the hospital fighting for his life. The second reason was because the police were out worse than I'd ever seen them all around Orange Mound. According to Mikey they had fliers up looking for me in connection with Bryon's murder, and the shooting of Bryon's brother. Not only that, Byron's people had rolled to the Mound that same night and Swiss cheesed my truck. Then cocktail bombed my apartment. I was devastated. They were coming for my ass in a major way. I still hadn't heard from Toya, and she hadn't tried to get into contact with Shantê either. I didn't know if she was alive or dead and to be honest, I didn't even know if I cared.

I spent my week drinking codeine and popping Percocet's. Every now and then I'd check in with Smoke to see how much he'd made, but because there was such a heavy police presence everything was moving slow around the hood. It was fucked up.

On the seventh day Mikey came and scooped me. Took me out to his duplex on Jefferson. It was right across the street from a Martin Luther King school. It was bright and sunny outside. The previous night it had rained all night so I could still smell the wetness of the earth.

When I made it inside his living it was already packed with like eight grimy looking dudes. They stood as we walked through the door. I went right to my waist ready to pull up my strap. I had a quick vision of busting that bitch until it emptied. I didn't know who they were, and I didn't have time to care.

Before I could up my pistol all the way every one of them came out with hand guns. They cocked them fast and aimed at us.

A light skinned, heavy set dude with freckles all over his face spoke first. "Say Dunn, call ya mans off daddy or we about to turn this bitch into a blood bath. Word is bond." He muttered, watching me closely.

"Fuck is this nigga Mane. Ain't never seen none of deze niggas in Memphis before." I was ready to squeeze even though I knew they would have gunned me and my right-hand man down. I got bad vibes from each one of those cats. They looked super grimy, with their long dreads, and baggy clothes.

"Man, all you niggas lower them guns in my mafuckin house. Y'all my cousins and this my brother. Knock this dumb shit off." He snapped mugging first them and then me because they lowered their guns, and I kept mine aimed ready to buck that high yellow nigga to the ground. "Phoenix. What the fuck I say Mane?" He placed his hand on top of my gun and applied just enough force to lower it.

I dropped it to my side. "Deze the niggas from Brooklyn that you was telling me about?" I asked, sizing them up.

"Yeah, they gon make up the body to this Duffle Bag shit. These my lil cousins. They hittas, and they certified head bussahs. I busted bunch of moves with them back in the Apple. They bout they paper just like us. They get my stamp of approval.

The light skinned dude laughed. "Yeah well you got ours for the most part, but kid was a lil shaky when it came to using them knives son, on what?" He cracked to his crew behind him. They laughed and shook up with a handshake that I had never seen before.

"Yeah, yeah, yeah. Anyway. This my nigga Phoenix. When you see him, you should see me. This my right hand, and he shoulder to shoulder with me in this Duffle Bag thang. Y'all telling me you wanna make millions, well me and the Homie gon oversee that and make sure that it happens. Phoenix this my cousin Korky. Dis nigga bout that life in every sense of the word. That's his brother behind him. His name Den-Den."

Korky extended his hand and shook mine. His eyes peered into mine. "Yo kid, you can put that cannon up, its all love up in here."

"Yeah Money. We don't up swords on each other. We murder all those that oppose us. Its the Brooklyn way." Den-Den was about five feet nine, high yellow, and about a hundred and sixty pounds slim. He had freckles all over his face as well. I could tell that he and Korky were blood brothers because of how much they favored each other.

I tucked my Glock into my waistband and pulled my shirt over it. "That's my bad kin people. Its just that old habits die hard." I started to shake up with all eight of them, and it was then that I found out that only Korky and Den-Den were Mikey's blood cousins. The other dudes rolled under those two, and according to them would die for Korky and Den-Den in a heart beat. That was cool with me just as long as we had Korky and Den-Den riding behind us. We needed some fresh blood from a different city, and with these New York niggas its exactly what they would provide. So, I got well acquainted with each one of them. I took a shine to Den-Den right away.

Den-Den was real quiet, but whenever he opened his mouth it was always to speak his mind, uncut or to ask a question that would further his knowledge of things. I could tell that he was hungry and ready to get his chips up. He was twenty years old.

***

Since Orange Mound was hot as a fire cracker, we took to hustling out of one of Mikey's traps on Park Street. We got money in front of the row houses. We stood in front of the buildings there while the sun beamed down on our heads making it feel like we were being cooked. Later, me and Mikey posted up in his Monte Carlo and served our bags from there facing Park Street. Park Street was just a few miles down from Orange Mound and I could tell that right away because it seemed like every dope fiend in the area was flocking to us to cop what we were serving. I was running out of Yay every two hours and so were the homies. Mikey was in charge of running in and out of his trap to refill everything. I stayed in the whip under the cool air conditioner. It felt good and did very little to keep my mind from racing.

About midway through the day, Mikey came back and refilled my pack. He laid his driver's seat back a lil bit and made a strange face. "Bruh, Alicia just told me that she pregnant."

I served the hype that was at my window. Gave her five bags, and she slid me a fifty-dollar bill. "There you go lil mama. I appreciate the bidness. We gon be right here all night long. Bank on that."

She smiled with yellow teeth. Her wig looked too small to her head. "Baby, I thought every time we spend fifty a round here that we get a bag for free?"

She placed her hand in her hip.

"Aw shawty, I ain't never heard nothing about that. But its good. Here go my cell number." I wrote it on a piece of paper. "And these two bags on the house. Make this number rang for me and I'll make sure you're straight. You feel me sweet heart?"

She took the number and smiled. "I'ma do just that lil daddy. You got my word. I sho don't mind earning a few of them down the road. Matter fact watch this big ass as I walk away." She smacked her booty that were encased inside of some tight, pink jogging pants.

I shook my head as she made her way across the parking lot. It was hot as hell. I knew that pussy had to stink. No thank you. I thought.

"Did you hear what I said bruh?" Mikey asked.

I stared to count my cheese. I had a healthy knot. Well over eleven thousand so far. "Nall Potna. Tell me again."

"I said that Alicia is pregnant."

"That's good. You should be rejoicing. What's the problem?"

"The problem is something ain't right I can feel that shit in my bones. I only been fuckin less than a month. How could she know that she's already pregnant? Do it work that fast?"

I shrugged my shoulders. "I don't know but I'm always hearing females say that they know their bodies, so maybe she just know already." I folded my thick knot. "When you say that you can feel somethin ain't right what do you mean?"

He pulled his nose. "I don't know Mane. Just something don't feel right. I'ma holler at shawty ass tonight and feel her out. That feeling in my bones rubbing me the wrong way."

"What is the feeling saying? That she cheating or something?" I zoomed into him. I needed to see if his facial expression changed in the least bit.

"Mane as much as I love shawty, if I ever found out that she was cheating on me I'd stank her with no hesitation. Don't nobody cross me and not lose their life Phoenix. You already know what the code of the streets is. We live by this loyalty shit. By honor. Integrity. That's my wife but if she ever tried to pull some dumb shit on me, I wouldn't have no other choice other than to send her on her way. To my uncle's oven she'd go." He chuckled. "She a good bitch, too. I'd hate that.

I imagined him stuffing Alicia in the funeral home's oven, while she screamed at the top of her lungs begging for her life. Thereby sentencing her and the unborn child inside of her to death. Damn that nigga Mikey was loonier then me. The one thing I couldn't afford was for him to ever find out that Alicia and I had fucked around behind his back. I saw that causing a divide between us, and then starting a war.

"Before I forget. Nigga we on tonight." He took the double cups from the middle of his console and sipped out of them.

"On? What you talking about?" I asked.

Another hype tapped on my window and slid a twenty-dollar bill through the crack of the glass. His lips were white as fuck. Like he'd kissed a handful of flour. He scratched his head, with his eyes bucked.

I took two of my biggest rocks and gave it to him. He jogged away as if he was in a rush to get ghost. When he got to the end of the parking lot, he took off running.

"Tonight, we bust this last move for the connect. Then this Saturday you finally meet them before we're blessed.

Its gon be sweet Phoenix, and don't think I forgot about how them niggas sweated you. I didn't. We just gotta handle one thing at a time. We can't be spread out like a promiscuous bitch in high school. We gotta focus on one mission at a time. But I did a lil digging. I know where them niggas are from. Remember that fool Dragon that I was hollering at you about?"

"Yeah what about him? You ready to sweat that nigga too?"

"Yeah, I am, in due time. But that ain't the reason I brought him up. I brought him up because of them fools that sweated you. You know Bryon's people? Well they run under him. They some important niggas in his crew. The one brother that you did smoke was his right hand, so its looking like sooner or later we gon have to take a good look at them anyway. But as for tonight we gotta put an end to a few niggas like the final scene in a movie. The pay is ten bands a piece, and an actual sit down with the plug. Both are beneficial right now so we gon make it happen. You wit me?"

"Until the dirt, Playboy. You already know what it is."

"That's all I needed to hear. Long as I got you having my back I ain't worried about nothing. We been potnas over a decade baby. That's why I'm pulling the right strings to make sure that we both pull ahead the way we're supposed to. Tonight, just follow my lead. Shit might get a lil messy, but its for the greater good." He held out his hand and we shook and gave each other a half hug.

"Its all love fool. Let's make it happen."

***

Vrrrm. Vrrrm. Vrrrm. Mikey revved the chainsaw once again. He held it over his head and looked back at me.

"Niggas don't think fat meat greasy, bruh. Hold that nigga arm. Pull it away from his body. Yeah just like that."

I took a hold of the Spanish dude's arm and held it out for Mikey. He lay back in the metal chair with his ankles tied together. His torso tied around the chair. Five minutes prior both me and Mikey had beaten him senseless with Billy clubs. Once again Mikey didn't let me know what this person's significance was in the grand scheme of things, but I just followed his suit. I didn't like doing shit blindly, but my back was against the wall. I had the law, and a bunch of angry niggas on the hunt for me. I was in a position that I had to depend on Mikey until I was in a position to where I could depend on my self. For as long as we'd been getting down and dirty together, he'd never steered me wrong, so I was down for the homie. I pulled harder in the man's arm. Held it straight out.

Mikey revved the engine of the saw again and brought the blade to the man's shoulder. Cutting through the meat and muscle there. His blood spattered all over the basement. He screamed into his duct tape. The sound of the blade screamed before slicing through him. His bound feet kicked in the air. The smell of burnt flesh and gasoline filled the basement. Sweat poured down the side of his face as his eyes rolled into the back of his head.

"You don't think fat meat greasy? Huh? You think this shit is a game?" He sawed into it some more and then all the way through it.

I was pulling so hard on the arm that I fell backward with it still in my grip. That freaked me out. I dropped it on the concrete and jumped up. Looked over to the Spanish dude. His arm was skeeting like a geyser.

"Mafuckas don't wanna fall in line bruh, this shit gon cost them an arm and a leg." He put the saw on the man's right hip and cut into his right leg. When it was all said and done, we wound up leaving him in the basement an arm and a leg short. It was one of the most gruesome things that I'd ever seen in my entire life. And something in my soul told me it was just the beginning. In order to make it to the top in the south we were going to have to get as grimy and gruesome as they came. It was time to put Memphis on the map.

Ghost

Chapter 10

Three nights later and I'd still not heard a word from Toya. I'd reached out to her aunt and she hadn't heard from her either. She had also been absent on all her social media platforms. That was unlike her. Something wasn't right. I was starting to think that Bryon's people had either killed her or were holding her hostage somewhere. What made matters worse was that Shantê was starting to ask about Toya and worry. I didn't like my baby girl being concerned with grown people problems. She was only eight. That wasn't right.

So that is what was running through my mind as the shower water beat into my face. I was set to sit beside Mikey and finally get the chance to meet the connect that was supposed to put us into the game. I'd turned off the shower, grabbed the terry cloth bath towel from the rack, and started to dry my body when Kamya stepped into the bathroom wearing a short pink wife beater with nothing on underneath it. I could see her nipples poking through the cloth. She had her long curly hair dropped behind her. Her edges were freshly brushed. She smelled like Prada perfume. She closed the door behind her and stepped inside. "Where you thank you finna go cuz?"

I continued to dry my body while looking over hers hungrily. "I got some bidness I need to take care of with Mikey. I'm finna get my chips up so I can do what I need to do."

She took a hold of my dick in her small hand, running her thumb over my dick head. "That sound good and all that, but before you go you finna hit this pussy. You might as well turn that shower back on and give me fifteen minutes of your time." She dropped down and stroked my dick. Kamya licked all over the top of it, then sucked me into her mouth, deep throating me with her eyes closed.

I fell back against the wall and rested my hand on top of her head., fuckin slowly into her mouth. Her suction got tighter and tighter. Kamya started making all kinds of slurping noises, breathing through her nose heavily. I groaned and exhaled loudly. "Damn baby cuz."

She popped me out and rubbed my dick all over her yellow cheek. Licking up and down the pole, she sucked each ball into her mouth, before deep throating me all over again at full speed. Her titties fell out of the side of her arm holes. Then she was pumping my dick again. "You ready to fuck me yet cuz? Huh? You ready to see what this young pussy be about?" She licked the length of me again, rubbing me all over her cheek.

I don't know what it was. But for some reason I had to taste that pussy. I was feening for it. I picked her lil ass up and sat her on the edge of the tub. I knelt between them thick thighs and sniffed her bald box. I mean I put my nose right on her hole, after spreading the lips. She smelled so good. Pussy smelt good to me period, especially that forbidden pussy.

Kamya moaned and pinched her clit, jerked, then held her lips apart. "I just put Shantê to sleep. She ain't gon bother us. You can do whatever you wanna to me. I'm down." She cupped her breasts in her wife beater.

I had them lips open wide, licking up and down her groove. She was already oozing. Everything that spilled out of her I slurped and swallowed. My tongue made revolutions around her pearl. I sucked it into my mouth and drank from it like a nipple filled with milk. This made her hump my face. She forced my head further into her lap, growling like a young Lioness in heat. "Uhhhhh. Phoenix." She gasped. More humping. Riding my face. "Tell me this pussy taste good. Tell me."

I was drinking, swallowing, licking and sucking her lips. My tongue fucked in and out of her. I was getting that pussy. She started jerking and clawing at me. moaning. Kamya wrapped her thick thighs around my head. Her perfect toes were on my shoulders and she came.

"Uhhhhh. Phoenix. Fuck. Phoenix." Her juices began to squirt out of her. They ran down my chin and onto my naked chest.

I was so horney that I was beating my piece. I had to fuck her. I could feel her spit along my shaft. She'd left it nice and wet like a young veteran. I laid her in the floor and got between them thighs. Without waiting I Placed my head on her puffy red lips and slowly eased into her heat. She was so wet that it made the task nearly effortless. I got three inches deep and was being seared by her heat when I felt the barrier of her hymen. "Kamya. I feel that down there baby. You sho you want me to break that shit. You better tell me before I do it." I ripped her beater down the middle and smushed her titties together, sucking the hard nipples, loving the taste of them in my mouth. When I nipped at the left one, she arched her back and moaned deep in her throat.

"Break it Phoenix. Take my virginity. Its yours. I been wanting you to take it since I was ten." She opened her legs wide and tried to pull me into her. I felt her lips wrap around my dick and I couldn't take it any more. It was feeling too good.

I cocked all the way back so that the head of my pipe rested on her small hole, then I slammed forward as hard as I could breaking through her protective barrier and landing in a wet oven. Her pussy was so tight that I almost came right on the spot.

"Aww shit! Unn! Phoenix. Fuck, fuck, fuck."

I got to plunging in and out of her box. Long stroking that shit on my grown man. I threw her legs on my shoulders and went to work watching her make some of the sexiest sex faces I had ever seen in my life. She bit

on her bottom lip and squinted her eyes. I could see hints of the light browns.

Kamya wrapped her arms around my neck. Breathing hard. Arched her back. "It hurts some cuz but fuck me harder. Fuck me harder. Hit this coochie." She sucked all over my lips.

My dick beat at her walls faster and faster. I dug deeper and deeper. She got wetter and wetter. I kept hearing all kinds of taboo shit in my mind telling me that I shouldn't have been fucking her. That I was bogus. That I should have given her a pass. The more I heard it, the harder I went. I took a hold of her small waist and beat that pussy senseless. I watched my dick going in and out of her pink goodness. I saw how her lips opened and closed around my wide pipe. Her ooze stuck to my sack and left a string of juices every time I pulled back.

She arched her back for the third time and came hard, screaming into the bath towel that I once wore. I slid between her legs and sucked on her clit some more. Fingered her at full speed until she came again.

"Get on your knees baby cuz. Come on baby, hurry up. Put that big ass in the air. I gotta have this shit from the back. You too strapped for me not too."

She got on her hands and knees and looked back at me. "You finna turn me out. You finna turn me out. You doing too much. I can't handle this shit."

94

I grabbed a handful of her hair and moved it so I could suck on her neck. My dick brushed up against her pussy lips. "Reach under your body and put this dick back in you. Hurry up. I'm finna grow yo lil ass right up since you want this dick so bad." I squeezed her perfect titties in my hands.

"Unn." She took my piece. "Its so heavy. Damn its so heavy." And put it into her self. "Shit Phoenix."

I gripped them small hips and got to stroking like it was going to be my last piece of pussy. It felt so good. So wet. So hot. That big ass booty warmed my stomach every time she crashed backward into me. It jiggled Every single time. Her breasts did the same thing.

She crashed backward into my lap faster and faster, bringing my tool under her spell. "Fuck me Phoenix. Fuck me big cuz. Uh. Uh. Finally. Finally. Yes. Yes. Finally. Aw. Aw. Aww. Aw. Yes. I'm cuming. I'm cuming! Phoenix! I love you!"

Our skins met in a steady, clap, clap, clap, clap, clap. I was hitting that shit hard. She smashed backward and that was all she wrote. I pulled my dick out and stroked him at full speed. In a matter of seconds cum started to fly out of the tip. It splashed on to her ass in big globs. I kept right on stroking. When I saw the way the mouth to her pussy remained wide open. That brought on a second orgasm from just the sight of that bald pussy.

She turned all the way around and sucked me into her mouth and started milking my nut from me. I ran my fingers through her hair, kissing all over her forehead.

Ten minutes later we wound up in the shower. I washed her body and she washed mine. Every few minutes we stopped and tongued each other down. That would lead to a lot of heavy breathing. Then she was bent over again with me fucking her hard from the back. 1 smacked that ass every few strokes. That pussy felt even better then the first time now. I couldn't get enough of it. I hit that shit hard too, with no mercy. We wasn't supposed to be doing what we were doing anyway. But since we were it was my job to tear that pussy up. So, I did.

***

After we finished and I came for the fifth time, I carried her the guest bedroom and laid her on the bed. She had her arm wrapped around my neck, exhausted. I laid her all the way back and kissed her lil naked pussy. I licked up and down the slit a few times, then laid beside her.

She moaned and opened her thighs wide. Her hand trailed between her legs, gripping her kitty. The fingers roamed through her cleft.

"You good lil mama?" I asked kissing her lips.

Cuz nodded. "So good. It was everything that I thought it would be and more. I love you so much Phoenix. Thank you for getting me right." She pulled me down to her and tongued me down. Kamya broke our kiss after two full minutes of tonguing and sucking on each other. I got up and got ready to leave. "Wait." She sat up. "What does this mean?"

"What you talking about?"

"Phoenix. This can't be the last time. It just can't be. We need to figure something out." She seemed like she was close to panicking.

I sat in the bed beside her. Rubbed her thick thigh. "Kamya chill. You good lil mama. We good. This ain't gon be our last time. I had just as much fun as you did."

"But I didn't do nothin. I didn't get a chance to show you that I'm not all the way dumb. You couldn't have enjoyed it." She started to shake.

I laughed.

"Its not funny Phoenix."

"Kamya. I got you baby. We good. You ain't must do much because this lil bald thang right here had it all covered. I'll definitely be back. You gon be my lil secret. You know what it is shawty. This Memphis."

Her eyes turned bright. She got on her knees and wrapped her arms around my neck. "I love you Phoenix. I love you so much. Please be safe out there." She hugged me tighter, then kissed my lips again hungrily, moaning heavily. Both hands traveled up and down my back.

I leaned back and kissed her forehead. "Its good shawty. Make sure you look after my lil one while I'm in these streets. I should be back in a lil while. You hear me?"

She nodded. "Please just be careful out there. I heard they got fliers all over the Mound looking for you. You already know how people are in Memphis. It's only so long before everybody will try to be a hero for the right amount of money."

I lifted my shirt and showed her the two handles to my burners. "If it look like a rat, and act like a rat, den I ain't got no other choice than to exterminate 'em. That's how that's gon go." I kissed her forehead again. "I'll see you later." I had money on my mind. A nigga was thirsty to see this new connect.

"Okay Phoenix." She crawled into the bed with her boy shorts all in her ass, then got under the covers.

Ghost

Chapter 11

Plucka. Plucka. Plucka. The big blades from the helicopter chopped through the air as we flew over the city of Memphis after midnight. The bright lights of the downtown district illuminated the night sky. From up here the city looked so beautiful. So serene, and like no death could come from it. I knew better. I'd been in Memphis long enough to know that only the stronger survived in this city. Without money, and power the average person in this city was nothing more than a rodent or a scum bag. I had to get my bread right. I was tired of feeling less then a man. I was hoping this plug was the real deal. We'd busted some heinous moves for them already, so I was already thinking that whoever this person was that they were sadistic in every sense of the word.

Mikey held out his fist, with the ear covers over his head that would prevent his ears from popping. They also allowed for us to communicate while the big blades made all that fucking noise.

I dapped his fist and nodded. I couldn't believe that I was flying in a chopper. I'd always hated heights. I never thought I'd have enough money to afford a helicopter or be so major that I be transported back and forth in one.

"This that shit right here ain't it bruh?" Mikey asked. His voice sounded like it was coming through a weak frequency. I had to adjust my headphones so I could hear him clearly.

"Hell yeah, nigga. I don't know who we bout to go and see Mane, but I likes how they getting down already. I could get used to some shit like dis."

"Me too bruh. That's what I was thinking." He dapped me again. "Don't even trip though. We about to get our chips right, and in a few years we gon be rolling the same way on a regular basis. Feel dat." Mikey promised. He pulled a blunt out of his shirt pocket and licked the length of it, then sparked it. "Ain't no way I'm not gon enjoy this experience wit out a lil Loud Pack.

The smoke sailed by to my nose and made me thirsty for a pull too. At the same time, I wondered what was good wit Toya. I still couldn't believe that she could set me up to be murdered in the way that she had. I understood a person being salty, but I was her daughter's father. That was the only reason that I'd given her so many chances and didn't smoke her on so many occasions even though I wanted to like crazy. Something wasn't right with her. I wish I had known that she loved Bryon the way that she did. I would have never done what I had to him in front of her. No matter what he was gon get what he had coming for putting his hands on Shanté. But I would have waited and handled my business when Toya was no where around.

Mikey tapped my shoulder. "Look nigga, that's where we about to land." He pointed to a big ass parking lot, beside a beige mansion. I scanned the entire area as the chopper began to descend and saw that the entire area was filled with mansions, and a lot of them had their own parking space for their choppers either on the side of their mansions, or on the very top. I was so used to being in the slums of Memphis that I didn't even know that areas like this existed. I was dumbfounded. "Damn we gotta get our green up. Them projects got a nigga trapped, Mane. Fa real."

Mikey nodded. "Not fa long Playboy. Not fa long."

A few minutes later we jumped off the chopper, and were escorted into the mansion by two big, black ass niggas. I didn't see their pistols, but I was sure they were carrying them. They led us downstairs into the main portion of the palace. We walked through a long hallway that was lined with paintings of Barack and Michelle Obama. Aretha Franklin and Prince. It smelled like jasmine. The temperature was cozy. Soft white carpet was beneath our feet Somewhere in the distance there were speakers playing the soft sound of jazz. The mansion made me jealous. It was nicely furnished. I could see myself living in a place like it and getting used to it right away. The mansion is what I felt I deserved. One day I would have one. I was sure of that. When we got to the huge living room the two guards pulled out the chairs from the table and Mikey and I took seats. The table looked long enough to seat twenty people. The room was dim and from here I could hear the Jazz ever so clearly. Mikey sat across from me with a stern look on his face. The guards stood behind my chair and made me feel extremely uncomfortable. We had been forced leave our weapons inside of Mikey's truck, so I felt naked and at the mercy of whoever this connect was.

Out of nowhere Mikey stood up. I frowned at him. He snapped his fingers and motioned for me to stand up as well. I waited a few seconds and slowly stood. As I looked to my right, I saw a big, muscle bound, black dude step into the room. Behind him was a blonde about five feet five inches tall. She looked to be about a hundred and twenty-five pounds and very pretty. Her bright blue eyes pierced my own when she looked over at me. She smiled weakly and stepped up to Mikey.

He held out his arms and hugged her. "Nastia, how are you Goddess?"

"I'm fine Mikey, baby. I've received the gifts and I take that to mean that each mission was complete as ordered?"

He nodded. "With no hesitation."

"And this handsome young man over here. Is he this Phoenix that you were telling me about?" She looked back at me.

"Yeah, that's my Potna. Me and him do everythang together. You want a crew to take over Memphis. We the crew and he gon sit at my right hand. This my blood right thur."

Nastia came around the table and stood in front of me. Up this close I could smell the heavy scent of jasmine. I'd never been this up close to a white female before. I felt uneasy. Memphis was kind of weird, and a bit racist so I didn't know what to expect. She must have detected that because a slight smile spread across her face. "What's the matter Phoenix? You look like you're uncomfortable."

This irritated me. "I'm good shawty. It's nice to meet you. You gon give me a hug like you gave my homeboy?" I held my arms open for her.

She looked me over and scoffed. Turned her back on me and walked to the front of the table. "Both of you have a seat. Now that you are here Mikey, and you've done everythin that I told you to do in a timely fashion, we can talk business. Let's discuss the Orange Mound. That's the turf you're looking for right?"

He nodded. "For now. Its good money in the Mound, and if you're about to put any crew in place there then it has the be the Duffle Bag Cartel. Ain't nobody gon put in that work like we will. Believe that."

She sat down at the head of the table. The dim light reflected off other red lips. Now that I could size her up from a distance, I had to admit that she was fine, and I had never been the type to fuck wit a white bitch. "How so?"

"Well I keep hearing the legend about that Rebirth raw that you manufacture. They say that shit is potent and make the dope fiends feel like they're getting high for the very first time every time. We gotta get our hands on that. If we can we'll shut down Orange Mound and slowly take over Memphis, crushing any other crew that stands in our way along the way. You already know how I get down. My Potnas are equally lethal. Trust me on that."

I was confused at why he was explaining his self to this white woman? Was she supposed to be the plug or something? And if so, how did she get on? The dope game in the south was cut throat. I couldn't see no woman penetrating it. Especially no white woman. But then again what did I know?

Nastia looked Mikey over for a short while. Then she gazed at me. "There are a bunch if crews that are looking to plug in with me. Some that have given me the same spiel that you are right now. They accrue large sums of money and have their priorities in check. And their right-hand man isn't wanted by the local authorities for suspicions of murder. Why should I take a chance on you when you carry around baggage like him?" She pointed at me with her chin.

That shocked the shit out of me. "Hold on shawty. Ain't nobody proved me guilty. That's just a bunch of rumors. That's why I gotta get my cake up so I can get me an attorney to fight these charges before the law even tries to bring me down. Everything we trying to do has a purpose. My lil situation ain't gon stop us from going hard for you and our crew first and foremost. Its all about the money, power, and respect."

She tapped her four finger nails on the table one at a time, eyeing me closely. She remained silent for what seemed like an eternity. Scoffed and looked over to Mikey. "You know what I demand Mikey. There are no second chances with me. You fuck up one time. and you're dead.

I kill you. I kill your kids, and everybody that has your last name because I don't deal with mistakes. I've been in this game a nice while now. I know how to survive it. I helped your uncle Tywain to become a legend. But even then, I never took pity on him. I refuse to take a chance on a man I'm only going to wind up giving the order to be killed. He has too much baggage. Baggage leads to problems. Problems lead to failed missions. Failed missions lead to me losing money. Lost money leads to lost lives. Generational massacres." She mugged me. "I'm sorry. No dice."

I wanted to call this bitch out of her name. To check her pink ass. How the fuck she got to her position of power was beyond me, but I didn't give no fuck. I wasn't about to allow her to talk to me like I wasn't shit. Nall. I was more of a man than that. I cleared my throat.

"That's Taurus's nephew right there." After saying this Mikey sat back and smiled.

Nastia stood up and bucked her eyes. "Is this true? Is Taurus your uncle? And I'm not just talking that ghetto uncle shit. I'm asking you if Taurus Stevens was really your blood uncle?" She watched me intently.

I nodded. "Yeah. My mother was his sister. Why? What's so significant about that?"

She covered her mouth with her hand. Her eyes got misty. Then she gathered herself and sat down. "Okay, I'll give you a chance Mikey. You and your crew. But I'm letting you know right now that I don't deal in second chances, and I don't accept excuses. You got one time to fuck up with me and its death. You understand that?"

Mikey sucked his teeth and nodded. "Hell yeah, I do. But what's good wit bruh's situation? You know he got them people on his ass. You think you can call in a few favors?"

She was silent. She looked over to me and smiled. "I think me and Phoenix is it?"

I nodded.

"I think me and Phoenix need to get an understanding. Once we establish that I'll determine how far I can go for him."

***

Later that night I had a million questions for Mikey, as we drove through the streets of Memphis. I felt that the first was the most important. "Say Mane, why the fuck was it so crucial that you brought up the fact that Taurus was my uncle? He used to fuck wit her or something?"

Mikey cruised in his drop top Lexus. It felt a bit cool out but not uncomfortably. "Mane her and Taurus use to more then fuck around. She got his daughter. Her name Natalia, and unbeknownst to you she used to go to school with us." He smiled and shook his head. "She was the lil mixed chick with the long curly hair that used to roll to the school in a Bentley all the time. Everybody knew damn well she ain't belong at King high, but ain't nobody fuck wit her either."

I started racking my brain. The only mixed chick I knew that drove a Bentley to our school had been a year behind me in the eleventh grade. She was about five five, with hazel eyes, and strapped beyond belief. Facially she was okay, and she took to wearing Chanel glasses. I didn't know if she needed them or not. I never tried my luck with her because I was too busy chasing them Spanish hoes in the school. I had a thing for them. In my opinion a bitch had to be bad and strapped, whereas Natalia was strapped, but she wasn't all the bad too me. Bentley or not.

"Yeah man. That was your cousin the whole time and you didn't even know it. Shid, I didn't find out until a few years ago when I ran into her at the mall. She got to hitting it off with Alicia and that came out. Shocked the shit out of me. So yeah, we got a definite in with Nastia because of you. I think she gon wanna holler at you on some one on one shit. You know just to make sure you're who you say you are. As long as you check out and you can prove that you are related to the legendary Taurus like I am Tywain, man shawty gon push us to the forefront of the game. That's where we need to be. Look at this." He pulled up to a red light and reached under his seat. Pulled a silver package from under it and set it on his lap. "Nigga do you know what this is?"

"Yeah that's a bird. I can't tell rather white or brown though." I felt the texture through the foil. It felt hard as a rock. There was red writing all over it.

"Nall this ain't just a bird. This is the Rebirth. This one brick will make us seventy-five gees nigga, and that's if we don't nickel and dime it up. Not only that, but this work will get the fiends hooked like fish on a line for good. Our uncles brought this shit to Memphis. They left it to shawty, and its our birthright to get that shit from her an to get rich off it. I'ma do everything that I can to find out the ingredients. When I do its over with." He pulled off. "This white bitch is the key to everything my nigga. This bitch finna put us on. She gon fix that lil police situation and everything. Watch."

Mikey sounded really confident, and because he did, I got to feeling the same way. I wasn't the type to put false hope into nobody, but it was just the way he looked when he talked about her that convinced me. He was all in, and so was I.

106

Chapter 12

Alicia hit me up three days after me and Mikey had spent two days straight getting the Rebirth aluminum foiled and bagged up. We were looking to push straight dimes. That way the feens could get just a taste of what we had to offer before we flooded the area with it. By the end of the second day I was tired and ready to go to sleep. But we went from bagging and foiling, to collecting all our bread from Smoke and his crew. Mikey had them spread out at a few traps in Memphis. He wanted to make a run to Jackson, Mississippi so he could pick up a few bricks of girly, but I declined. At the same time, he was hitting the road with Korky to make that trip, Alicia was hitting my phone saying we needed to meet up so we could talk.

I met her at nine at night on a rainy Saturday. I knocked on the door to their apartment, and she let me in after a few minutes. I rushed past her and into the house. Happy to be out of the rain.

"Dang, I ain't know it was gon be raining like that. Had I known I would have met you somewhere that was half way. I'm sorry." She took my coat and hung it on a coat rack.

I stomped the rain from my Jordans in their door mat and took them off altogether, along with my fitted cap. "What's good Alicia? You made it seem like its an emergency."

She guided me toward the couch. "Have a seat Phoenix. Can I get you something to eat, or drink?" She stepped half way to the kitchen, looking at me over her shoulder. She wore a night gown that stopped just above her knees. As usual, that ass was poked out like a beer gut. She was on bare feet. Her pretty toes had French manicures to them.

"Shawty bring me a shot of that syrup. I know Mikey got some of that shit lying around somewhere." I grabbed the remote from the table and turned on the big television that was hanging on their wall. I saw that whoever had been watching the television before me had been watching the Raised as a Goon movie. It was paused. I pushed play and sat back.

Mikey and Alicia had this apartment decked out with expensive furniture, and leather couches. Across from me a fireplace was roaring. The wood crackled loudly. I could smell the scent of burnt wood. Alicia stepped back into the living room shaking the bottle of Sprite up and down. "I don't know of you like yours shook up, but Mikey do. If not, I apologize. Here you go Durty."

I took the bottle and twisted the cap off. "Dis the only way to get that shit mixed right shawty." I turned the bottle up and swallowed it in big gulps. It was strong just like I liked. The medicine taste was heavy. The aftertaste was even worse|. I couldn't help smacking my lips. "So, what it do boo?"

She blushed and sat on the loveseat across from me and crossed her thick thighs. Her night gown rose just enough to show the under side of her left leg. The skin looked soft, juicy, and forbidden. "I don't want you to freak out, and remember I'm just telling you this because its your right to know. I don't know how this is going to effect things, and I'm scared to look that far into the future. But Phoenix I love you. You're my big brother. You have a major piece of my heart, and you always will. And..." She lowered her head, then stated to bite in her index finger.

"And what? Why you stop there?"

She sighed. "Phoenix I'm carrying yo baby, and I'm scared half to death to tell Mikey. I know that is going to be catastrophic for everybody, but I don't know what to do. And I'm freaking out." Alicia covered her face with her hands.

I got up sat beside her and placed my arm around her body. "Damn, that's heavy Alicia. I mean something like that crossed my mind, but I didn't think too far into it. How many months are you?"

She uncovered her face. Her eyes were misty. "I'm twelve weeks. Keep in mind that my wedding night was barely a month ago. That was the first time that me and Mikey had ever been together. Sooner or later he's going to add up the dates. When he does, he's going to kill me. I love him so much Phoenix. I don't want to lose this good man. This world is too cold for me to be out there all alone trying to raise a child. Man, y'all dudes got it so easy. All y'all gotta do is fuck something and its over with. Meanwhile us women get the short end of the stick at every turn. We're the ones who are left with the child, the dilemma, the drama, and at your mercy unless we can fend for ourselves which in most cases in the ghetto we can not. These white folks ain't even trying to give us section eight or food stamps if a man is anywhere involved in the picture. Its designed for the black woman to fail at all costs. And that stinks." She covered her face again.

I rubbed her back. "Shawty I don't know why you writing me off as a dead beat, but that ain't in my nature by no means. If you got my seed inside of you I'ma definitely hold you down. Shid even if it wasn't my baby, I'd make sure that you were good. I care about you Alicia. I always have." I kissed her cheek and continued to rub her back. Even though I wasn't focused on it I could feel that she didn't have a bra on. I imagined what them titties looked like the last time I'd seen them. Caramel colored, with big, dark brown nipples.

She turned to face me and wrapped her arms around my neck. "What am I gon do when Mikey puts the pieces of the puzzle together? You know he gon kick me to the curb for sure. That's if he don't kill me first."

"He ain't gon kill you. That's my nigga, but you my baby mother. Ain't no nigga about to put his hands on you in no way."

"But that's my husband Phoenix. I love him. We ain't been married a month. I'm so bogus for doing this to him. We both are." She sat back and looked me in the eyes.

I moved her hair out of her pretty face and wiped away her tears. "So, what do you advise?"

Alicia shrugged her shoulders. "All I need to know is that you got me if he does kick me to the curb when he finds out. Just make sure I'm good until I can get on my feet. Be a father to your child. A damn good one at that. We don't have to be together. This is all I ask. Can you do this?"

I nodded and sank to my knees. Slowly kissed her thighs one at a time. "I got you Alicia." More kisses, moving toward the inner portions of them. "I got you. I'm not gon let him hurt you. I'm not gon hurt you. However, you need me I got you. I'm not trying to fuck up nothing that y'all got going on. To be honest you ain't gotta say nothing to him at all if you don't want to. I'll support you in either way. I'ma make sure my baby straight though. And you too." More kisses. That codeine was fuckin wit me. That and her scent. I missed Alicia's pussy. I wanted to see if I could get some while she was all vulnerable and shit. I licked along her inner thigh and kissed the crotch of her pink panties. Her lips made a prominent indentation inside of them. It looked so good.

Alicia rested her hand on the back of my head. "What are you doing Phoenix?"

I had to think fast. I was feening for that cat between her legs. I kissed the crotch with a bit more force and yanked the panties to the side. Her dark brown lips popped out, freshly shaven. "You're my baby mother now Alicia. That mean I got a stake in this pussy too. I been crazy about you since forever. I ain't trying to break up no happy home. You know I can keep a secret." I licked her box, spread the lips, and moved my tongue up and down her groove swallowing secretions of her essence.

"Unn. No, stop. We can't do this Phoenix. You promised. You promised that when I got married that we would be done with doing this shit behind his back. Oh! Baby! You promised."

I pushed her knees to her chest and got to eating that pussy hungrily. I had her lower lips wide open. Her slippery pink exposed. Me darting in and out of it.

She held my head. "Uh. Uh. Uh. Uh. No. Stop. Uh shit. Stop Phoenix. Stop. This ain't right. Uh." She threw her head back moaning.

I had two fingers going in and out of her pussy at full speed, while I sucked on her jewel. She was so wet it was like she was peeing in my mouth. I loved it. Swallowing every chance I got. I could feel that forbidden juice running down my throat and it drove me insane.

"Phoenix! Phoenix! I'm cuming already. Uh shit. Damn you. Damn you!" She fell backward.

I sucked harder on her clit, fingering her in a blur. She shook and moaned loudly. Juices ran out of her hole and on to the seat cushions below her ass. After she came hard, I licked all over her thick thighs. All the way to her calf muscles sucked them, and trailed even lower to her pretty toes., sucking them one by one. Wasn't nothing like a bad sista with some pretty ass toes. A bitch feet had to be right or I wasn't fuckin with her, and Alicia's were one hunnit all across the board. I sucked them toes with lust. Then I stood back and dropped my pants stroking my piece. "Suck this Alicia. Come on baby." I slipped my hand between her legs and started fingering her pussy again. My thumb was running from side to side across her clit.

She jerked. "Ugh. You get on my nerves Phoenix. You know how I feel about you, but I'm married now." She sucked my dick into her mouth and got to handling her business, while my fingers continued to go to town in her kitten. She was laid sideways suckling away. One leg raised. Her pussy was so wet that it was making noises.

I pulled my fingers out and licked them clean. My eyes closed as she brought me so much pleasure that I was on the verge of cuming. I couldn't let that happen. I had to have some of that pregnant pussy. I had to see what that was about now that I knew it was my shorty she was carrying.

I pulled out of her mouth, stroking my dick. It was covered in spit. I got between her thighs, and lined my dick up with her puffy labia, and slid into her silky, scorching cave.

She sat up and moaned. "Awwww, no. I'm married now Phoenix. I'm married."

And because she was, I got to long stroking that pussy like a complete animal. I was obsessed with that taboo shit. Mikey was my nigga. I loved the homie with all my heart. I'd fucked Alicia about twenty times before this time, and it had always been good. But since I was fucking my right-hand man's wife it made the pussy feel ten times better. I

112

think I was cursed with that forbidden shit or something. It ran heavy in my bloodline. I remembered how good Alicia had looked on her wedding day and imagined that I was fuckin her in her wedding dress. I got murdering that ass. Pushed her knees further to her chest, and watched my dick go in and out of her lil box that was dripping wet and making all kinds of noise.

Bam. Bam. Bam. Bam.

"Unnnn. Unnnn. Slow down! Uh-fuck! Phoenix! Phoenix! Phoe-NIX!" She started to shake like crazy.

I kept pounding. My seed was building up in me. I held the side of the couch and gave her ten hard strokes. Growled out of breath, and came as hard as I could, splashing her womb. We fell to the floor, me kissing all over her lips, and neck. I pulled her gown strap down and exposed a succulent breast and trapped the nipple in my hungry mouth.

She rubbed all over my chest, breathing heavily. "We gotta stop Phoenix. We gotta stop this shit right now." She pulled me down and we got to tonguing each other.

I gripped that fat ass and pulled her body to mine. She felt hot. My hands ran all over her lower back. Then I was cuffing her ass again. She felt so soft. Her scent rose to intoxicate me. I sucked her neck. "You're my baby mother now. You belong to me Alicia. Don't get that shit twisted. You hear me?" I licked all over her neck.

"Yes Phoenix. Yes. I hear you."

"Don't tell Mikey nothing. When the baby come just say it's premature. Bruh won't be none the wiser. You'll see." More sucking and licking all over her. Then I was back between her legs pounding away at that pussy.

Ghost

Chapter 13

Another two weeks passed. Me and Mikey found ourselves held up in the trap outside of Orange Mound hustling hard. In two weeks, we'd made fifty bands a piece, that wasn't including the paper that Smoke and his crew were making for us with the white. This was strictly the Rebirth money that Nastia had supplied us with. Originally Mikey projected that we'd only make something along the upper end of seventy bands, but we were just above a hundred stacks, and I still had a zip to go. Our dimes were small barely above a nickel, but the work was so potent that the fiends were running back and forth copping them by the hundred sack. Our trap was jumping like double Dutch.

Mikey came from out of the back room with a fist full money. "Nigga I told you that in no time we'd be eating like fat bitches at a buffet. Was I lying?"

I'd just finished counting fifty-three thousand dollars by hand. "Hell nall, you wasn't. This Rebirth is popping. That white bitch need to quit playing and hit us off right. That way we can flood the Brooklyn chapter of our crew, and Smoke nem. If we can get this Rebirth into everybody's hands that is working for us, we'll be rich in no time. What's the hold up with her?"

Mikey bent the knot and put a rubber band over it. "We should be getting a shipment in Wednesday night. The only thing is that before we do, she wanna holler at you. Alone." He bucked his eyes and sat across me, untwisted the cap to his drank and turned it up.

"Fuck she wanna holler at me about?"

He shrugged his shoulders. "I don't know, but she did me the same way. I think she just wanna pick your brain a lil bit. Either way you ain't got nothin to worry about. Y'all

115

basically family. Maybe she want to properly introduce you to your cousin. I mean who knows man?"

I was stuffing my pockets with money. I didn't know what she wanted with me, but I sure ain't have no problem finding out. If she had me lining my pockets like this in a matter of weeks, then I could only imagine what getting a good understanding with her would feel like. I was most definitely gon use the whole Taurus being my uncle as a crutch with her, especially since it seemed like she had a weakness for him.

"Man, we about to take this city over, bruh. You know we gotta holler at them niggas in Black Haven for that dumb shit they pulled with your whip and baby mother. The fire done died down a little bit, so I'm thinking we wait a week, and make 'em taste these fully automatics. What you think?"

I had a heavy heart for Toya suddenly. Nobody had heard from her in nearly a month. I was sure that she was dead. How could she not have been? "Bruh I say we keep getting this money first. Shawty say its gon make a few moves to get the law off my back. I wanna get in good wit her so she can stand on her word. If she dead set on putting us in the game, then the last thing we need to do is to be beefing wit a bunch of bum niggas. You feel me. If anything, we could let Brooklyn handle them chumps. Its money over Bitches. And that's all them niggas is a bunch of bitches. I smoked two of em already. No sweat off my brow." I finished stuffing my pockets and stood up. "Tell shawty I'm ready to meet her whenever she's ready. The sooner the better. In the meantime, I'm finna go check on Shantê. I need to spend some time with her."

"Yeah, that sounds like a plan. I need to spend some quality time wit the wife too. Gotta get in the habit of

116

talking to her stomach. That way I can develop a relationship with my child while its still in the womb. Man." He sighed. "I can't wait until that baby is born. I'ma give it the world Phoenix." He rested his hand on my shoulder. I stood up and hugged him even though I was feeling some type of way. I felt jealous that he was preparing himself to be a father to my child. Wondered what things were going to be like after the baby was born? If he ever found out the truth, I was sure that one of us would lose our life. I had to get as rich as I could with bruh before we became mortal enemies over the baby that was brewing in Alicia's stomach. It was most definitely inevitable. For the time being I would play my roll. I had to think about Shantê. "Bruh its a beautiful thang. That's why we gotta get our money right now before the baby come. Its like you said before, we can't be in these streets forever."

Mikey hugged me tight and stood back. "Now you see what I meant when I was saying that a few weeks ago. These streets is short term. We gotta think long term. So yeah, you gotta work yo magic on shawty."

***

That day, when I got back to Kamaya's crib, she was all over me on some super emotional shit that threw me for a loop. I had never seen her so emotional before. As soon as the door opened Shantê ran full speed into my arms.

"Daddy. Daddy. Daddy." She ran and jumped into my arms, hugging me as tight as her little arms could muster.

I planted kisses all over her face. Fell to the couch with her. "Hey baby. More kisses All over her pretty face. "I missed you too. You wanna go shopping?"

Kamya stomped her foot. "Okay. Okay. Its my turn. Don't forget about me Phoenix. Damn." She reached for my wrist and tried to pull me up.

I sat Shantê on the couch and embraced her. Before I could turn my head, Kamya kissed my lips. Sucked them. Then hugged me. "Damn I been feening for you all day. It seems like you been gon forever. I hope you know I'm coming shopping wit y'all." She kissed me again.

Shantê turned her head side ways in curiosity. Then she straightened up and frowned. "Don't be kissing my daddy. He's mine. Not yours."

Kamya rolled her eyes. 'Did you hear what I said Phoenix?"

I laughed. "Yeah, I heard what you said lil cuz. Its cool. We gon all roll out. I wanna hit you wit a few fits too and get you right. Come on."

Shantê stood up and crossed her arms in front of her. "But I don't like nobody kissing on my daddy but me, and not like she did. Yuck." She stuck her tongue out of her mouth and close her eyes.

I laughed again.

"And daddy, I don't want nobody going wit us because we haven't had a father daughter day by ourselves in so long. Its not fair. It makes me mad." She mugged Kamya on her jealous kick.

Kamya rolled her eyes for the second time and picked up her purse from the couch. "Well luckily for us you you're only eight and you're not an adult. I'm coming Shantê, so get over it."

Shantê hugged my legs, and I picked her up. She wrapped her arms around my neck and stuck her tongue out at Kamya. "Stupid, that's why when I grow up I'ma beat you up. Go find your own daddy. He's mine."

Kamya, stepped to the side of me. "Are you driving, or am I?"

Both had me cracking up, and Shantê kept going on and on from the back seat, while Kamya drove and I slumped as low as I could in the passenger seat.

***

"Aw hell yeah Durty, I like dis Prada dress right here, Mane. Dis show off my whole figure." She turned her back to the full-length mirror, checking out her ass, and the way the dress conformed to her body, while I did the same thing from a few feet away.

Shantê sat on the side of me sipping from her strawberry milk shake. She stopped and looked Kamya over. "That dress looks ugly on you. Maybe you should wear it on your head." She snickered and put her straw back into her mouth.

Kamya glanced over to me and smiled. "Well we're getting it along with the others because I can tell that somebody likes it here." She licked her lips and turned her ass to me and popped back on her legs. The dress rose just a bit. That ass was poked all the way out. We made eye contact in the mirror.

I winked at her to send my stamp of approval. If she wore the black and purple number around me, I knew for certain that she wouldn't have it on for long. I was already imagining doing some things to her that I had to shut out of my brain. I damn near forgot Shantê was there, until she got my attention.

"Daddy I don't wanna sit here and watch this dookie head try on stuff. I wanna go and get me some more stuff because I seen all that money in your pocket. So, can we go now?"

"Just a few more minutes baby, and we will. Okay?" I kissed her forehead.

"Okay."

Kamya tried on a few more dresses and we wound up getting all of them. Before it was all said and done, I'd allowed for them to run in and out of a bunch of stores. By the time we came from the mall I had so many bags that it looked like we'd gone grocery shopping on food stamp day. I wound up blowing fifteen thousand dollars. I felt stupid, but at the same time seeing the smiles on their faces was enough for me. As a hustler nothing made me happier than to be able to make sure that the defenseless people in my circle were well taken care. I'd blow a bag on my daughter any day. And since I was fuckin with Kamya the long way, I had to make sure that she was good too. It was my joy. Money wasn't shit if you couldn't make your people happy with it.

After the mall Shantê wanted to go to Dave and Buster's so she could play a bunch of video games. I gave her a Ziploc bag full of quarters and watched her run from one game to the next with a big smile on her face. "This is the best day ever daddy!" Shante exclaimed.

Kamya slid behind me and kissed my neck every time Shantê turned her back. "I can't wait till we get home and get her to sleep. I wanted you to fuck me as hard as you did last time. My pussy been feening for you ever since you pulled out of it." Her tongue licked along the thick vein on the side of my neck.

"Shawty, I can't wait neither. But you better chill for my baby catch yo ass and wild out. You already know how jealous she is." I cupped her juicy ass and kissed her lips briefly.

120

She shuddered. "Damn I can't wait Phoenix. You got that magic stick, Durty, and I need you to perform your act on me." Kamya said this in my ear all sexy like. Then stuck her tongue inside of it.

As Shanté finished her game she turned and saw how close Kamya was up on me. She stepped away from the arcade and grabbed my hand as she mugged Kamya. "Daddy can you play the rest of these quarters wit me? I'll have more fun if you do." She pulled me away.

Kamya flared her nostrils and took a seat at our table and crossed her thighs, pulling out her cellphone. She gazed up to me once, then went back to doing what she was doing on her phone. I could tell she was heated.

Shanté and I ran all around the massive arcade restaurant playing whatever games that she wanted to play. I completely allowed her to wear herself out. After three hours of that, I was carrying her out the door in my arms.

When we got home, I undressed her and slid her into the new pajamas that I'd bought for her. I put her in the guest bedroom, and tucked her in, after kissing her on the forehead. "I love you Princess." I looked my daughter for a few moments and got up.

When I made it into the hallway Kamya was all over me. She pulled my shirt over my head, then my black beater before starting to undo my pants. "Man, I want you to fuck me so hard Phoenix. I been playin wit my pussy ever since the last time you touched me. You done turned me out. I swear you have."

I stepped out of my pants. She dropped right down and took my dick into her mouth, sucking it hard. Kamya's head moved back and forth in my lap until she had me nice and hard. She hopped right on my waist, yanked her skirt all the way up without any panties on, and slid down on my dick. She was jumping up and down on it while I held her against the wall pounding that pussy out.

Her teeth sank into my neck, then she was sucking me there and moaning loudly. Her pussy was wetter than a tub of water. "Huh. Huh. Huh. Huh. Huh. Huh. Yes. Yes. Yes. Huh. Un. Un. Yes. Aw fuck yes."

I gripped that ass and brought her down hard over and over, digging deep in that pussy. Her tight oven was sucking me like a mouth, begging for my release.

She hopped higher and higher. Three her head back and moaned. "Uh! I'm cuming. I'm cuming. Aw shit." She got to shaking so bad that we fell to the floor with me still long stroking her faster and faster, punching them soft guts.

"Yes. Yes. Phoenix. Phoenix. Yes baby. Aww-oh. I love you so fuckin much." She started to hump her hips into me at full speed.

I curled her into a ball and went to work like a savage grunting and slamming into her box wit no mercy. Kamya bit into my shoulder which encouraged me to go harder, and deeper. Her hallway felt silky, and hot. The walls sucked at me. My nuts slapped against her ass as I dug into her body faster and faster.

She arched her back, and pulled me down by the neck, kissing my lips. Then her mouth was wide open breathing harshly. "Uh, you're killing my young pussy. You killing this young pussy. I ain't ready. I ain't ready." Then she was cuming again.

This brought my climax on. I pulled out and came all over her stomach. She rubbed it into her box, with her thighs wide open, breathing heavy. "I love you Phoenix. I love you so fuckin much."

Chapter 14

Nastia decided she wanted to meet up with me three weeks later so we could put some things into perspective. She told me that it was cool if Mikey tagged along because there was a proposition for the both of us, pending that everything checked out with me. I didn't know what that meant in its entirety, but I was all for it. I heard the word proposition and was ready to go. Nastia was a powerful woman. I was sure that whatever she had up her sleeve would pay off and be well worth it.

In three weeks, time me and Mikey had taken off with the Rebirth. We'd gotten shipment of eight bricks and them bitches were going harder than an old man popping Viagra. I was at a hundred and fifty gees from my cut alone and seeing that I was only taking thirty five percent of pure profit because my other fifteen percent was being reinvested back into our business, I felt that we were making a nice lead way. Smoke and his crew were eating because of us. Korky and his Brooklyn crew were eating just as much. We had both crews rocking with the Rebirth and the Girly so we could go twice as hard. Shit was looking real lovely.

Mikey opened the shops that he'd been telling me about all along. It was a sight to see him convert his illegal money into something positive and start to do the things that he'd sworn he'd do. That motivated me to come up with my own plan of action. I didn't know what I wanted to do yet, but every day I was thinking about it.

I picked up the bottle of Moët, and drank from it, took a puff from the Loud that I was smoking, and sat back in the soft, peanut butter, leather seat of the private jet that we were flying on. I felt like a boss. I looked out window at the clouds as they floated by our window as we cruised through the air.

Mikey took two Percocet Thirties and dropped them into my champagne. "Mane I'm fucked up. I been popping these bitches all night. A mafucka felt numb all over. He popped two into his champagne as well.

I placed my thumb over my Moët and shook it just enough to ensure that it would dissolve the pills. Then I was taking the liquid down any throat gulp after gulp. I wiped my mouth with the back of my hand and burped all rude and shit. "This bitch got us flying on a G-7 my nigga. This living."

"I told you bruh. Shit about to get real. I don't know what she got on her bird, but whatever it is that shit is done." He chugged his liquor, and frowned, lowering his head.

I detected something was wrong. 'What's good Play-boy? Why you looking all sour and shit?" I looked him over closely. He looked sicker than a mother at her child's funeral.

Mikey exhaled loudly. "It's my wife Mane. Something ain't right wit her and I can tell. She got that baby growing inside of her and everythang. Belly starting to protrude, but still she seem off to me. I'm worried about her." He took a swallow from the liquor.

I scanned the small jet. There were six open seats. Directly in front of us were a pilot and a security guard that Nastia sent to make sure we were straight. I was strapped and wasn't worried about shit. Mikey was too. If push came to shove, we'd gun asses down wit no hesitation. "Bruh I think all women go through that situation when they pregnant. You might just be making way too much of the situation. Just continue to support shawty and make sure she

124

taking them vitamins and thangs. Dats all you can do for right now. You feel me." The Perks kicked in. I felt numb, and high as the roof on a twenty-story building.

"Yeah Mane, I guess dats what I'ma have to do. Sides, all diss worrying ain't getting me nowhere but stressed out." He took another long swallow. "Bruh I know we don't get into all that lovey dovey shit, but I just wanna let you know that I love you. I'll kill for you my nigga. You the only true family I got, bruh. I can't wait until we blow them Black Haven niggas away for dat shit they pulled. Mafuckas still ain't seen or heard from Toya ever since then. But its good. They gon get theirs." He held out his hand.

We shook and then hugged. I was numb as hell. My eyes were low, and my heart was beating faster than a rock and roll drummer on steroids. "I love you too, mane. You all me and my baby girl got. That's why I'm ready for us to get this money together. We gotta make some shit happen. I'm tired of being broke, and I'm tired of the same ole same ole. Yeah, we seeing paper now, but I'm talking riding our own G-7s. Taking trips and spoiling our be loves without having to worry about the cost of shit. I can't wait until we get there.

"We'll be there in a minute, Boss. Trust a nigga on dat."

"Hope so. Mane I'm numb as fuck. I gotta close my eyes for a minute. I'ma fuck wit you in a few hours." I closed my eyes and drifted off into a far away land.

***

Ten hours later we stepped off the jet and on to the island of Honolulu Hawaii. It was nine in the morning when we got there. We were ushered into a black and gold Rolls Royce. The interior was all white leather. There were seven-inch televisions in the back in the head rests, and one in the dash up front. It we nice and spacious. The driver took us to the Waldorf Astoria hotel, where Nastia had two of her, big, beefy, bodyguards escort us upstairs to her Penthouse Suite at the very top of the building. We were in the elevator so long that I got nervous and thought we were trapped.

When it dinged, the doors opened and in front of the elevator was another beefy security guard. He led us down a short hallway, took a key out of his pocket and placed it inside of a digital keypad. The guard punched in a series of numbers before the big door in front of us opened.

I stepped past him and into a suite fit for a king. The first thing I saw was all white carpet, and a long table with a fruit basket filled with kiwis, pineapples, grapes, watermelon, apples and oranges. There were big bay windows all around with a clear view of the mouth wash colored ocean.

Nastia appeared from the back room dressed in a white Burberry cheer leading skirt dress that clung to her slim figure and big breasts. "Welcome gentlemen, come on in and make yourselves at home." She waved away the security guard. "That'll be all for now." The security left the room and closed the door behind them.

Two thick ass Hawaiians came from the back of the suite with Burberry robes. They walked up to me and Mikey and handed them to us, after placing their Hawaiian reefs on our necks. "Aloha, we hope you have a nice time here in the Island." Each of them gave us kisses on both cheeks and returned to the back of the suite.

Nastia hugged Mikey. "Good to see you baby. Anything you need my girls will take care of you. Don't hesitate to ask. We'll talk business later. For now, enjoy yourself."

"To be honest I just wanna catch up on a few zees until I can catch up wit this lil bit of jet lag. Where can I lay my head?"

She clapped her hands, and both Hawaiians appeared. "Take him to one of the rooms that have been reserved for him. Massage his body. Make him feel good. Treat him like a king. He is my guest. You understand?"

They nodded and hooked their arms into each one of Mikey's. "Right this way sir we're going to make you feel really good."

They headed toward the back. The grass skirts around their waists swishing from right to left exposing their rounded asses. I didn't even know that Hawaiians got that thick. They looked good, too, all bronzed and shit.

"Y'all can't massage on me too much. I'm happily married. He slid his arms around their small waists and glanced back at me. "See you in three hours, Mane." They disappeared into the back.

Nastia came over to me and took my hand. "I need to talk to you Phoenix. Come on, follow me." She walked slightly in front of me, her ass waving from side to side. She smelled like jasmine. When we got to her master bedroom, she pulled me inside, and closed the door behind her. She laid her back against it and sucked on her bottom lip. "Sit down on the bed."

I did. The bed was huge. Behind it was a big window that gave us a nice view of the Island. It felt like we were floating in the sky. "What's up Nastia?"

"So, you're Taurus's nephew. Damn, and I thought all the males of his entire bloodline were wiped out. But look at you. You are gorgeous?"

"I'm what?" I raised my left eyebrow, confused. Gorgeous was a term that I used to define a bad ass bitch. That word was too feminine for me.

Nastia sucked on her bottom lip, and slowly made her way over to the bed. Once there she stood in front of me. "Do you know who I was to your uncle?" Her tongue traced her lips.

I decided to play the fool. "Nall, me and him wasn't close like that. I might have seen him maybe fifty times when I was little. I heard he was a legend though."

She opened my legs and stood in between them. "Your uncle was a legend because of me. He was the love of my life. The only Blackman that I've ever been crazy about to this day."

"So, who were you to him?"

She took a deep breath and shook her head. "Your uncle saved my life not once but twice. The first time was from his sadistic brother, Juice, and the second time was the most important because he helped me to fake my own death. It was the only way that I could break away from my father, who was in control of some lethal Russians. They wanted me dead after they found out that I was pregnant with a Blackman's baby." Nastia gazed off into the distance. "Yeah, but Taurus took care of him, and then he helped me to break free unbeknownst to everybody else. There was nobody like him. Not now, not ever." She straddled my lap. The skirt rising on her hips.

I held her and looked up and into her pretty face. "That's cool, but how can you say that when you haven't met everybody. That's my uncle. We share the same blood." I slid my hands up and rubbed all over her lil ass, squeezing the soft cheeks. She wasn't strapped like I was used too, but that ass still felt hot. I'd never fucked a white bitch before but this one had a lot of power so if I needed to, I would fuck her brains out. I didn't give a fuck what she was to my uncle. I was focused on my advancement. Shantê had to have everything. I was in charge of that.

She placed her forehead against mine and looked into my eyes with her blue ones. "You think you can do me like Taurus used to? Huh? If you can do that, I'll make sure that you and Mikey are the richest niggas in the south. You can quote me on that." She rubbed all over my chest.

Man, I know damn well this white bitch ain't just call me and my dude a couple niggas. That shit almost made me push her off me. "Shawty I don't know what my uncle used to do, but I know what I'm capable of. We can figure this out right now." I pulled her skirt all the way up to her waist, exposed her G string, and ran my fingers under the string and into her gap. Her pink lips were bald, and thick.

She pushed me back. "Let me see something first. I have to make sure that you're authentic because Taurus was strapped, and so was Juice."

Damn she fucked Juice too? What type of shit was my uncles on? I wondered.

Nastia unbuttoned my pants and pulled them down my thighs and off. Next came my boxers. When she saw my dick, she shuddered, picked it up with both hands and sniffed. Suddenly she was stroking me. 'Its beautiful. Damn this is nice. I was praying for a son, but God had other things in mind." She licked the length of me, and sucked my dick into her mouth, pulling the skin back, tightening her fist as she sucked me faster and faster. Then she popped it out. "You wanna be powerful? You want to be a king? Then I'm your Queen. I'ma turn you into what I wanted to turn Taurus into but couldn't because my father was alive. Now I run things and I need you in my life." Her mouth swallowed. She was sucking me so cold that my toes curled. It was heavy with spit but before it could ooze down to my sack Nastia sucked it back up and was slurping at full speed.

It felt good, but I didn't know what the fuck she was talking about. I was my own man. There was no way I was about to live in another nigga's shadow. Fuck that. I was a boss at heart. I pulled down her shoulder straps to release them titties. They spilled out, all tanned and shit. The nipples were rosy colored. big, and covered a nice portion of the mound when they were fully erect.

She stood up with her fist around my dick stroking it. "Suck them Phoenix. Suck these white titties."

I leaned forward and I sucked them boys into my mouth one at a time, squeezing them together. They were nice and heavy, warm, and smelled like jasmine. I nipped at the nipples with my teeth. Then took them into my mouth, one at a time, sucking them with vigor.

She tossed her head back and moaned loudly. "Oh, yes. I gotta have some of this cock. I just have to. Come on baby." She straddled my lap and climbed aboard, leaning, her hard nipples into my face, and slowly slid down on to my pole, swallowing me whole. "Uhhh! Yes, that shit feels so good. It feels so good baby." She glided up and down. Her tunnel felt hot and swampy.

The tanned breasts rubbed against the side of my cheek. I had my eyes closed whole she bounced up and down on me. This was my first time fuckin a snow bunny, an older one at that. Nastia looked every bit of forty, give or take a few years. She dug her nails into my shoulders, and bounced higher and higher, throwing her blond hair all over the place.

I held her hips and made her ride me harder and faster. The queen size bed rocked up and down. Her moans got louder. "Ride this dick, bitch. Ride this black mafucka." She groaned and came hard. "Awwww yes! Yes! Talk that shit to me. Uh. Uh." She was riding me so fast that her hips were a blur. Her pussy was so wet that my entire lap was drenched in her fluids. "Fuck me. Fuck meeeee-yuh!" I flipped Nastia's ass on to her back and grabbed her by the throat. Then I threw her right leg on my shoulder and started hitting that pussy as hard as I could. I mean I was killing that shit. Making sure I was going as deep as I could, before pulling all the way back, and slamming it back home hard as fuck. I wanted to touch her inside of her stomach. Whatever she ate last I was trying to touch that shit.

Her big breasts wobbled and shook on her chest. The right one rubbed up against the silk sheets as I killed her pussy. "Yes. Yes. Aww fuck. Yes. Harder. Fuck this cunt harder. Oh, shit I love it. I love it, Taurus." She screamed with her eyes closed tightly.

Taurus? Really. No, this bitch wasn't thinking about my uncle while I was ten inches deep in this pussy. That would have been a shot to the ego of a lesser man, but I had a hidden agenda. I needed her plug. I needed her influence. I needed this bitch to get me rich. If she wanted to imagine that I was my uncle while I was all up in this ass, then so be it. "Gimme this pussy Nastia. Fuck me back baby. Uh, fuck. I missed you so much. I missed this pink cunt Nastia. I missed it so much!" I sped up and started hitting that shit so hard that I was hurting myself. I saw how it looked for my black dick to shoot in and out of her pussy and it was mesmerizing. I was hitting that shit so hard that her cat was swelling up. All kinds of juice was pouring out of her. This sight affected me in such of way that I felt myself beginning to cum.

She sat all the way up and tried to kiss me. No suh. I pushed that bitch back and sped up my pace before I pulled out at just the right time and came all over them pretty ass tanned titties. She rubbed it in like lotion, then grabbed my piece and sucked it into her mouth draining me.

Chapter 15

Not only did Nastia somehow, some way get the police to get off my ass, but there was no longer a warrant out for my arrest.

Apparently, some other nigga that had been caught red handed for two murders and a bank robbery confessed to the shootings that I'd taken part in. I didn't know how he could do such a thing when I knew I was guilty of the offenses, but Mikey said that's how street politics worked when you were fuckin with bosses. And Nastia was most definitely that. Just because the police were no longer pursuing me for those murders didn't mean that Bryon's people weren't.

Toya was still missing in action. Nobody had heard anything from her, and four months had passed already. I was worried, and ready to make a move on those Black Haven niggas. It seemed like every time I got ready to out a plan in action, Nastia had a mission lined up for me and Mikey that we had to accomplish right away. Though each mission was lucrative, I was beginning to become annoyed. I felt shackled and smothered by the powerful Russian. In a matter of months, she'd become obsessed with me. Openly at that. She'd admitted that shit to Mikey and me on more than one occasion. I didn't know what to do other than to keep giving her this black dick.

On the flip side, she plugged us with the Rebirth. The Rebirth was the most addictive, and chemically enhanced heroin that anybody could come by. In order to get it you had to go straight through Nastia and her connects. She was real particular about who she put in the game with it. But lucky for me and Mikey she gave us the green light, and we were going harder than an erection.

Since Mikey had his Brooklyn boys doing the most for him, I decided to snatch up Smoke and his crew of eight. Nastia hit me with eight bricks of the Rebirth. Nickel and diming it up, I was set to make eighty bands off each one totaling a hundred and eighty thousand dollars, easily. That was the mission, so I had the lil homies aluminum foil it up just like that. We snatched up three trap houses right inside of the Mound and got to going crazy. Once the dope heads found out that we were pushing the Rebirth it was a rap. In a matter of a few days they were forming long lines to get served.

There were two main twelves that walked the beat of our section of the Mound named Links and Jack. Jack was a dark skinned, tall copper with a bald head and bad breath. His partner, Links was just as tall, but he was white. The first time they saw the dope line leading from our trap they respectfully made their way through the crowd, until they were at the front if it. Once there they knocked on the door, just as I was pulling up in my brand new black on black 2020 Range Rover that Nastia had brought for me just out the blue. When I saw them, I jogged to the front of the line, and asked the officers to step aside.

Jack mugged me, on the hot summer day. Beads of sweat dripped down the side of his face, and from his chin. "This your lil operation here?" He asked.

The line continued to go on about their business. That was one thing about the feens in Memphis. They didn't care about the police or nobody else. They minded their own business and carried on about their day. Smoke and my servers continued to sell bags as if two officers of the law were not standing right amid everything.

"Yeah Mane, this my lil spot and we need to conduct a lil business. That's my bad for not hollering at you fellas ahead of time. I know y'all run this shit." It was in my best interest to stroke their egos. On the low, I didn't give a fuck about neither one of them pigs. My first step was going to be to get them on the payroll, and I hoped they played ball. If they did not, then step two promised to be ugly. I didn't mind smoking one, or both. I mean I didn't want that heat, but at that same time I was making thirty thousand dollars a day in cash. That was on a bad day. In my opinion any life was at stake if it prevented me from making that kind of money.

Links surveyed the line and shook his head. "He gots to be making every bit of twenty grand out of here a day. Look at this shit. Its ridiculous."

Four more people came and stood in the line. Smoke's crew walked up and down it shouting orders to keep the line straight and single file. They threatened that if anybody had a hard time following those commands that they could leave and never return. I could make out the butts of their guns poking from their shirts and I was sure the officers could as well.

A short distance away, a bunch of little boys were throwing a football back and forth to each other. A ways from them five little girls were playing hopscotch. It was so hot outside that I could literally make out the waves in the atmosphere. It had to be every bit of a hundred and five degrees.

"What you need to talk to us about?" Jack asked sizing me up. "We got enough evidence right now, along with your admission to take you to the precinct. And if I can recall there was just a warrant out for your arrest a few months back. Somehow the order was taken back. You must know somebody that knows somebody, boy?"

I scoffed. Here we go with is boy shit. In Memphis whenever somebody called you a boy that was a major sign of disrespect. It was equivalent to being called a ho, or a bitch nigga. When a white person, or the police called you that it was a fancy way of them calling you a nigger, or something along those lines.

"Say we ain't gotta do all of that boy shit. Clearly, we need to get an understanding so that both sides are happy here. So, if you will, please let's take a walk."

"Yeah, right to the squad car. Let's go, sonny boy." Links added and took a hold of my arm.

I allowed this to happen. The only thing that spooked me was that I had two nine millimeters on me, fifteen thousand in cash that I was going to use to pay Smoke with, and in turn he would pay his workers, and about a quarter zip of the Rebirth. If they wanted to be petty, they could pat me down, find everything, and take me in for a long time. If that happened, I would've been fucked.

They led me to the squad car and put me in the back seat. Smoke ran out of the trap with his hand under his shirt. "Hold the fuck on Mane. What y'all about to do wit the homie?" He yelled.

"Get back! You get back right now you little muthafucka or I swear to God I'll turn you into target practice?" Jack yelled, pulling his service weapon out of the holster and aiming it at Smoke.

Smoke mugged him, and slowly backed up. "Yeah, aiight Mane. Hit my phone when you need to make bail big bruh. This that fuck shit wit these people Mane. I hate you sons of bitches!" He snapped.

Jack returned his weapon and got into the driver's seat. Behind him the long line continued to get their work and keep it moving. "Boy you lucky I don't go out there and

136

break that line up. How much would that cost you for the day? He grunted.

Links laughed. "Those addicts would be right back as soon as we pulled away. My sources tell me that they're using a mix so potent that the addicts are coming all the way from Black Haven just to get a taste. You stepping on a lot of toes, Mr...?"

"Just call me Phoenix." I said wondering why they hadn't patted me down. I could pop both in the back of the head and get away with it if I so chose to.

"Nall we gon call you doing Fed time if you're not trying to play ball." Links quipped. "Now what do you wanna talk to us about?"

"Money. What else could we have in common?" I looked at the back of their heads as they pulled out of Orange Mound.

"Money." Jack joked and tapped his partners shoulder. "And just how money are we talking?"

"Well, I know y'all ain't making shit but thirty to forty thousand a year. The pay is not worth the job. If you fuck wit me, you ain't gotta do shit but stay out of my way. Let me do my thing for a few months, and for the inconvenience I'll pay you five a piece every week. In two months, you'll make your entire salary that you would have made with the department."

Links looked over to Jack and then back to me. Motherfucker are you dumb? You think we're going to accept a measly twenty grand a month when you're making that in a day. You gotta be kidding me. Either you double it or kiss our asses. Find yourself a new spot to infect because we're going to evict you from this one."

I was prepared to give them twenty a piece. I was making more than that everyday. But when it came to the game and haggling you were always supposed to start low and negotiate from there. Because I had used that tactic, I was saving myself ten gees a week. "You know what, even though that's going to hurt me a bit, I gotta do what I gotta do. Ten it is. Here go five a piece right now. I'll give you the other five this Friday. From every Friday on out I'll have the twenty. All I ask is that you keep me wit a heads up. Protect your investment and respect my hustle."

Jack stopped at a red light and turned around his seat. "Sucka, you're still on your own. All that money gon buy you is breathing room from us. Orange Mound belongs to me and this man. We're your land lords. Keep us right, and we'll see to it that your stay on our turf is as habitable as possible. But when it comes to the other animals that will be looking to devour you soon, our hands are tied. We'll protect you from the law, but not the streets."

"Yeah you got that home boy?" Links asked.

I counted out ten bands and gave them five a piece. "The last thing I'm worried about is the animals of the streets." I meant that shit.

***

A month later, I sat beside Mikey at his trap in North Memphis and counted five hundred thousand dollars in cash by hand. By the end of all of that counting my head was pounding like it was being struck wit a hammer. I loaded my money into my duffle bag nice and neat, and zipped it up. Just as I was getting up to grab me a bottle of codeine so I could add it to my Sprite, my phone buzzed, and Toya's picture popped up on it. At first, I thought I was seeing things. I hadn't heard from her in so long that I just knew it couldn't be true. I stood up and mugged the phone as it continued to ring.

138

Mikey gave me a what up nod. "Fuck, what wrong wit you?" He asked crushing two Perks sixties on a silver platter.

"Dis my baby mama right here, Mane. I ain't heard from her ass in almost six months." I didn't know what to do.

I felt like I had a bunch of butterflies in my stomach. I didn't know if I was more worried, or angry that she'd been gone for so long.

"Playboy, answer dat mafucka. Ain't no sense in that bitch to keep on ringing. Find out what's good wit shawty monkey ass. She got a whole ass daughter wit you." He said, before lowering his head and taking a line to the dome.

I nodded, put my ear piece into my ear, and answered the phone. "Shawty where da fuck you been? You got my daughter all worried about you and shit, Mane. And I bet not find out that you was the one that tried to have me killed."

The phone was quiet on the other end. After a moment there was laughing that came from a deep voice. "Say Potna, this ain't no muthafuckin Toya just yet. You see, me and you gotta talk some bidness before you're able to jam wit that bitch again." He said.

"Mane who da fuck is dis?", I snapped.

Mikey tooted his last line and stood up. "Fuck going on, Bruh?"

"Dis Black Haven muthafucka. Just because you got the law off yo ass, that don't mean you don't owe the hood. Mafuckas hear you out there getting it now. Large quantities, and bundles of cash. Well if you wanna see your daughter mama again, you're about to come off a lot of that shit. I mean the mafuckas around my way is starving. We need to eat my nigga, and the only way we about to sit at a buffet is if you and yo right hand set that bitch out before us. That's how shit finna go."

"You got me fucked up nigga. I don't negotiate wit bum niggas. Fuck you and all of them niggas over there in Black Haven. Sides, how I know my baby mama ain't already dead?" I hollered into the phone.

Now Mikey was mugging me. "Put that shit on speaker, Mane. Let me hear what the fuck they talking bout. Sound like they on some extortion shit."

"Yeah put this bitch on speaker because I got something to say to his bitch ass too."

I pulled out my ear plugs and flipped the phone to speaker. "If you got Toya nigga let me hear my bitch right now." I encouraged. My mind was racing like two sprinters in the Olympics.

"Say Mikey, I got yo thick ass mama too, and ya pops. We was tryna get that pregnant bitch of yours but mafuckas ran out of time. Soon though. The fee is a million a piece nigga. You got two weeks and I better have my shit. I'ma text both of you fuck niggas the time and the place to drop my shit off at. Come late on my scratch and I'm whacking this old bitch first. Now try me. I'ma be in touch." The phone went dead.

We both stood dumbfounded. My heart was pounding in my chest. I didn't know what to think, or what to do. I looked my phone over stupidly.

Mikey picked up his phone. Scrolled down the call log and hit his mother's number on speaker phone. It rangand-rang. Then he called his father's line. It did the same thing. "Mane, this nigga gotta be bluffing. I know this nigga ain't got my mama and daddy, Bruh. My people don't fuck wit nobody. Come on let's roll out to my mama crib. She stay twelve blocks away. If this nigga touched my peoples, Mane. I'm bout to blow Black Haven off the map. Believe that, like a true story." He headed for his trap house's back stairs.

I could feel that the next chapters of our lives were about to be full of drama and chaos. I grabbed my jacket from the back of the couch and followed him outside and into the pouring rain.

Ghost

Chapter 16

"Aw hell nall, Mane!" The lightning flashed across the sky as Mikey ran up his mother's front porch steps and took them two at a time. The front door was wide open and hanging off the hinges. He pushed it aside and ran into the house.

I was a short distance behind him. Thunder roared in the sky like an angry lion. The rainfall intensified. The steps were a bit slippery, but I did what I could to keep my balance. Then I was inside and running behind the homie.

When I got inside, the house was in shambles. The living room table was turned upside down. The China cabinet was shattered. There was glass all over the carpet, along with muddy footprints. We rushed into his mother's bedroom. It was empty. The bed had been flipped on its side. We came out of there and met up in the kitchen. There were broken dishes all over the floor. The refrigerator was pushed over, and the cabinets were open. A lot of the food that had been inside of them was now on the kitchen floor. There were busted open cereal boxes, and the deep freezer's contents were also all over the floor.

Mikey mugged them for a second, and then frowned. "Aw shit Fam!" He opened the back door and took off running down the back steps.

I looked all around the house. It looked like somebody had been searching for something. But why the fuck would they have been looking for something inside of Mikey's mother's crib? She was a Christian woman. A Queen that stayed to herself. I didn't understand."

Mikey came back upstairs with a mug on his face. "The got me bruh! Them bitch ass niggas got me for my scratch!" He snapped.

"What." I looked him up and down. "Fuck is you talking about Potna? You just left the crib earlier wit a duffle bag.

"Behind the washing machine bruh. I had one point six million behind the washing machine, in the wall. Somebody hit me. That was all the bread I had to my name." My eyes were opened so wide that they hurt. "One point six muthafuckin million. Seriously?"

Mikey lowered himself down to one knee. His head hung low. "That was me and Alicia's nest egg for the baby. Now I ain't got a pot to piss in, and these niggas got my parents, Phoenix. What the fuck am I going to do?"

"Man, you betta get yo ass up. Fuck you mean what you gon do?" I pulled his ass to his feet. "We about to roll over here to Black Haven and bring that heat bruh. I'm talking shut that bitch down. They got my baby mother, your parents, and your cheese. Nigga ain't nothing left to be talked about."

Mikey looked sick. "Somebody had to know where my stash was. Somebody had to tell them that I kept all my scratch at my mother's house. That's the only way they could have known."

"Yeah but who. Who did you tell?" I asked looking him over closely.

He shook his head. "You already know I ain't that fuckin stupid. Only person knew was my wife, and she'd never get down on me like that." He rubbed the hairs on his chin, lost in thought. "A muhfucka must have been watching me close. I been too lax, that's what the problem is. Yeah, but its a wrap for all of that. I'm about to make these niggas feel the noise. Let's ride out my nigga."

I grabbed his wrist before he could brush past me. "Nigga hold the fuck on. You acting like you might know who did this shit? If so let me know what's good?"

He stopped and frowned. "Its Bryon's people, but even more so, it's that fuck nigga Dragon. That pussy nigga had a thang for Alicia, mane. Ever since we tied that knot, I been feeling the vibes coming from that chump. If a nigga playin the game like dis it's in my best interest to take a good look at him before he can put my money to use. So, let's ride out."

I stood there a moment, before I followed behind Mikey. I didn't know who the fuck Dragon was, or what he was to Bryon's people, but I was about to find out.

***

I slammed the clip into the Mach Ninety, and cocked that bitch and adjusted the black leather gloves on to my hands. Next, I leaned back in my seat, taking a strong swallow from the bottle of syrup. I was high off two Mollies, and a Perk thirty. I was feeling venomous, ready to lay some shit down.

Mikey pulled into the back alley and threw his Buick Century into park. It was a dump off car. A nineteen ninety, black on black, with rust spots all over the door. He pointed at the house. "That's where Dragon lay his head. Its him, his baby mother and his two sons. He think because he chill out in the burbs that he ain't gotta face this music? Man, I'm finna spit so many lyrics at his ass with this Mach that he gon think he on The Voice."

I pulled the Donald Trump mask over my head and adjusted it so I could see out of the eye holes. Once my vision was straight, I was ready to go. I was worried about Toya, but at the same time I didn't know what to think or expect.

For all I knew she could've been a pulling the strings behind the scenes.

I hopped out of this Buick and jogged down the alley. It was really storming out by this point. At the same time, it was scorching hot and humid. There were mosquitoes every where. I didn't know how that was possible, but it was horrible.

We ran down the alley, and along side the garage that was behind their house. Then we ran through the backyard., along side of their gangway, and I stopped in front of their patio door, nodding at Mikey.

He stepped forward with a huge brick, that he'd gotten from the alley. After setting his Mach on the ground, Mickey held the huge brick over his head, and with what seemed like all his strength, he tossed it through the glass patio door. The glass shattered, loudly.

I kicked the door in the rest of the way and rushed inside ready to wet anything in sight. My eyes zoned in on two little boys that were making a run from the living room. They appeared to be about five and six. They ran yelling for their mother.

Mikey was on their asses. He snatched them both up and clunked them in the back of the head with his gun. They fell to the floor. Out colder than two bears during hibernation season.

A female with a bath towel wrapped around her body appeared at the top of the stairs. When she saw the kids on the floor, she screamed. "Don't hurt my babies. Please don't hurt my babies!"

Mikey aimed at her. "Bitch get yo ass down here right now. Get down here or on everythang, shawty I'ma lace yo ass."

146

She held up her hands. "Look Mane. You got me. Just don't hurt my damn kids. They babies. They ain't got no beef wit you, Playboy." She slowly made her way along the banisters and then down the stairs with her hands above her head. She was partway down the steps when her towel fell from around her caramel body, revealing her nudity underneath. She was bad, a bit chubby, but fine.

Mikey met her half way and grabbed her by the hair. He drug her down the stairs and tossed her on the floor beside her children. He put the gun to the back of her head. "Punk ass bitch! Where the fuck Dragon at?" He forced her face into the carpet.

"I don't know, Playboy. I swear God I don't know. He ain't been here all day long. Last time I seen him was yesterday. He came home and gave me a knot of cash and left back out without saying a word to me. Said he'd be back in a few days. He was getting some things right. I didn't know what that meant, and I didn't ask him. Very rarely do I question him about the streets. I stay in my lane."

Most of her explanation was muffled because of her face being stuck in the carpet by Mikey. She cocked her right leg the rib, and her cleft was exposed. Her cat was trimmed and meaty.

"Yeah well Bitch you about to come wit us. You and these punk ass kids. That nigga took some things that belong to me, and until I get all of them back you and your kids gon feel the wrath of a nigga. You got that?"

She sniffled. "We ain't in dem streets Homeboy. That's between you and they daddy. You need to leave innocent folks out if dis." She turned all the way around and looked up at him.

"Nall bitch." Mickey pressed the barrel to her forehead. "You bout to call this nigga right now and tell him that we got you and his kids. That if he don't give me back my parents, and my money, then I'ma smoke each one of you muthafuckas before I come and get him. That's what you gon tell that nigga, mane. You got me shawty?"

"Look, I'll tell him whatever you want me too Just don't hurt me and my kids."

"Fuck yo cellphone at, bitch?" I asked, scanning the living room.

"Its on the kitchen counter. Right next to my Benz keys.

I grabbed her Galaxy off the table and handed it to her. She turned to her side and sent him a text. Begging him to pick up the phone. After the text she added the number twenty-three. "Y'all just hold ya horses. He gon get right back go me, trust me. I know my man."

Mikey grabbed her up by the hair and drug her across the carpet toward the back door. "Mane grab them kids, bruh. Everybody going in the muthafuckin trunk until we figure this shit out." He picked her up and tossed her on his shoulder like a rag doll.

I snatched up both kids. We wound up forcing them into the trunk while we waited for Dragon to respond to the message that his bitch had sent to him. It was crazy because Mikey stayed parked right behind their house with the phone on his lap taking toke after toke of the Loud. "I'm letting you know right now that I'm not accepting this shit, bruh. That nigga gone release my people. And he gon give me my cheese. If he don't I'ma cut they heads off, and that a be that. I'ma come up with that one point six again. I ain't worried about that. Its the principle of the whole thang." He took a long swallow of his drank until he downed the entire bottle.

I hit Toya's phone again. It was my eighth time doing it. I was hoping that she picked up just so I could know that she was alive. I cared about Mikey, but I was finding it real hard to go there with him emotionally over his people, and his money. I needed a horse in the race so to speak in order for me to wanna go hard. That's just how the killer in me worked.

The phone buzzed on Mikey's lap. He put it on speaker. "Man, where the fuck is my bitch, and my kids, Mane?" The same voice from earlier snapped.

"Bitch ass nigga where the fuck is my peoples, and my cheese? I ain't about to play wit you. You fucking wit a live wire Potna. I'll wipe yo whole bloodline off this earth from fuckin wit me and mine. This that Duffle Bag shit, boy."

"Say Mane, I ain't fuck wit no kids doe boy. I could a snatched yo pregnant bitch and that fuck nigga Phoenix lil punk ass daughter, but I chose to leave the bitches and kids out of this. You about to make me turn up doe."

"Shut yo bitch as up." I snapped. "Nigga let everybody go and we can shoot this shit out like souljahs. Me and my nigga versus the whole Black Haven for all I care. What you think bout that, Homeboy?"

"Say Mane, my bitch pregnant. My sons innocent. They ain't got nothing to do wit none of this shit. You let them go, and I'll let yo momma, and yo daddy walk scot free. This bitch, Toya owe the mob for getting my cousin beat to death, and my other cousin smoked. We can't take that shit lying down. Far as that scratch nigga, respect the game. That shit ganked. Its Black Haven's now."

"That's yo word nigga?" Mikey asked sliding his hand over his Mach.

"That's my word." Dragon returned. "Ain't no hoes over here. What we gon do about our peoples?"

"Just wait I'ma sho you." He opened the driver's door and got out of the car. "You fucking wit the wrong nigga bruh. I'ma show you real good."

Chapter 17

The rain was pouring like crazy. It pelted the concrete loudly. Mikey popped the trunk of the Buick and snatched Dragon's baby mother out of it by her hair. He slung her to the ground next to the open driver's door and straddled her body, then reached into the car and grabbed the phone. "Say nigga, I got yo bitch right here, Mane. I'm giving you five seconds to tell me that you gon hand over my peoples and my cheese. If you neglect to, I'm finna smoke this bitch and both boys. Then if I gotta personally knock on every door in Black Haven until I find your punk ass, I will. These problems you can't stand my nigga, trust me. Now beg for your life bitch, while I count to five." He forced the phone to her ear. "Beg bitch. You better think about them lil boys back there."

"Dragon, please don't let him do this to me, baby. Please. We're innocent. We don't have nothing to do with what goes on in the streets. Please give him his stuff back." The rain poured onto the back of Mikey's head, and Dragon's baby mother's face.

Mikey took the phone from her. "Here we go nigga. One. Two. Three..."

"Nigga you touch my bitch and you gon start a war. Get off that bitch shit. Face me like a man!"

"Four. Muthafucka five!"

"Nooooooo!" She screamed.

"No mercy, bitch." He pressed the barrel to her face and squeezed the hair trigger. *Taaat. Taaat. Taaat.*

She shook as the bullets entered her forehead. A sea of blood formed under her. Some of it sailed down the alley mixing with the rain water.

Mikey stood up and grabbed the phone. "Its war nigga. Its muthafuckin war." He popped the trunk and bucked inside of it. *Taaat. Taaat. Taaat. Taaat. Taaat. Taaat.* The gunfire illuminated the alley. He took the boys and threw them into the alley and slammed the trunk back. Mickey came and got in the driver's seat. "Come on bruh, we gotta get rid of this car. Then we gon go holler at them niggas in Black Haven. I'm bout to go door to door about mine."

As the car was peeling away, I took one final look into my rearview mirror at the slain bodies in the alley and shook my head. Any hopes that I had of ever seeing Toya again slowly faded away.

***

An hour later we poured gasoline all over the car, and torched it, in the back of the old car place on Normandy. Then we pushed it into the creek, after allowing it to burn for an hour.

"Lets go holler at these niggas, Boss. On everythang. We can't give Dragon and his people no breathing room. They working wit a million dollars and some change. In a street war you could do a lot with that. We can't be on the receiving end right now. There is too much at stake. I'm finna text the Brooklyn Fam and see what it do." He started to text.

I pulled away rolling his Ford Expedition. There was a bunch of shit on my mind. I wondered if Toya was dead, or was Dragon waiting to kill her? After what Mikey had done, he had every right to body her and his parents. The homie had taken things too far if you asked me. I needed to get to my daughter to make sure that she was safe and sound. I was even thinking about moving her out of the city for a little while. At least until things died down. I had to protect my baby.

Mikey hung up and kept a mug on his face. "They ready to move. Our niggas say its whatever." He cringed and shook his head. "What the fuck was I thinking, Phoenix? I might've just killed my parents." He clenched his jaw. "This codeine fuckin me up, Bruh. I should've thought shit through thoroughly."

I shot daggers at him. "What nigga?"

Mickey rested his hand on his forehead. "Damn, I just fucked up. I might have just killed my parents, Phoenix. That's my mama. My old man. Aw shit." He sat all the way up and shook the cob webs from his brain.

"Say, Mane, it's too late for all that remorseful shit. You just stanked Dragon's Bitch and his three kids. Its, war and that's it." I assured him.

"Three? Fuck you getting three from?"

"You smoked both of his sons, and his unborn child. That's serious. One hunnit percent that fool bodied your parents, and probably my baby mother, too. We ain't got no other choice other than to go all out."

Mikey's phone rang. His mother's picture appeared on the screen requesting to Snapchat. He accepted the message. "Here go my mama right here."

I pulled over to the curb. As soon as it came on Dragon had her by the neck. She was buck naked. He held a Machete in his right hand. "This what you want, Mane? Huh? This what you want muthafucka?" He raised the machete in the air.

"Look away Mikey. Look away." I tried to grab the phone from him, but he held it out of reach and tilted it so that we could both see the action unfolding on the screen.

"I gotta see this shit, bruh. Gotta release that beast inside of me." He said, frowning. Dragon took the big knife and brought it down into Mikey's mother's face as hard as he could. I watched long enough for the blade to make contact, and then I looked away as he went into a murderous rampage on the screen hacking away at her.

"This. What. You. Wanted nigga? Huh? Is. This. What. You. Want?" Harder, faster hacking. It sounded like he was going to town on her.

I glanced back at the screen. Dragon continued to beat her senseless with the blade. Tears rolled down Mikey's cheeks. He nodded his head. "That's all I needed to see nigga. Trust me, that's all I needed to see." He turned the phone off. "Bruh, drop me off at the crib so I can get my wife straight. I'ma have you swing back around and snatch me up in a few hours. That sound cool?"

I couldn't even make eye contact with him. "Dawg you awright?" I knew it was a stupid question, but it was the only thing I could think to say. I could only imagine that he felt like shit. He and his mother were really close. I wasn't really too sure how he felt about his father. We simply never talked about him.

"Its all in the war, right?" He shrugged his shoulders.

"Right." In the back of my mind I was thinking that he'd brought this one on his self. There was no way that he should have done what he had. That had to be all that dope fuckin wit him.

Mikey wiped the tears away from his face and sighed. He turned on Meek Mill's *Championship* album. He nodded his head to it and leaned back. I didn't know what was going through his head, but I could only imagine.

***

Mikey grabbed a bottle of Patron from f his refrigerator and turned it up with tears rolling down his cheeks. He was guzzling loudly then he stopped and shook his head hard. "I fucked up man. I fucked up. What was I thinking?" Alicia came into the living room and stood beside me. She kept one hand placed on her stomach protectively. What's the matter with him, Phoenix? What did he do?"

Mikey took the bottle away from his mouth. "I killed my mama, and probably my daddy. Then I lost our nest egg. I fucked up baby, but I'm finna get our shit back. I'ma make 'em pay for what they did to my people, baby." He turned up the bottle again and drank nearly half of it.

Alicia looked over at me in fear. "What is he talking about Phoenix? How did kill his parents?"

Mikey staggered into the living room. He was drunk as an alcoholic on payday. "See, Dragon stole my stash, and took my people. So, I killed his whole muthafuckin family. *Bam. Bam. Bam. Bam.* All four of them. Them bitches had to go. So, I sent 'em on their way." Mikey made his fingers into a gun, then he pulled out his handgun from the small of his back and cocked it. "But it's cool, I'm ready to go to war." He slurred his speech.

Alicia looked worried. She took a step behind me. "I won't never seen him like this before Phoenix. Maybe you should get him out of here until he come off whatever he's on. I don't feel safe in here right now."

"You don't feel safe? How the fuck don't you feel safe?" He took three steps forward and finished the entire bottle of Patron and threw it to the ground, shattering it.

Alicia was behind me fully now. Her nails dug into my sides as she cowered behind me. "Please baby. You need to get some sleep. You been up the last few days trapping.

Den, you just drank a while bottle of Patron. You're not in your right mind right now." She said with a shaky voice.

"Right mind. Right mind." He aimed the forty five directly at her after pulling me out of the way so he could get a straight line to her. "Bitch, you probably the reason that nigga went to my stash spot. You the only one that knew that I kept my shit in a big ass hole behind my mother's washing machine. Yeah that pillow talk done got a nigga in trouble, ain't it?"

Alicia closed her eyes. "Mikey, you are real high, and real drunk. You need to take that gun and put it back into your waistband. You're talking real stupid right now."

"Stupid. Stupid. Bitch ain't nothin stupid about me. I peep everythang. I just play dumb. You don't think I know that you're way too far along for that to be my baby?" He said this through clenched teeth. Mickey grabbed her by the shirt and pressed the gun to her temple.

Now it was time for me to intervene. I stepped on the side of him. "Mikey that's your wife, man. Dats yo queen right thur. You gotta treat her as such. You know damn we'll she ain't fucked off on you. That gurl loves you Mane."

"Nall she don't. She just like everybody else. This bitch got a hidden agenda. It was all about my bread. That bitch ain't shit but a rat looking for my cheese. Now she got it Potna. All one point six million of it. Bitch gotta give me mines or eat this lead. I already got my mother killed. I might as well lose everybody in one day." He curled his lip. Where my bread at Alicia and whose baby is that?"

She swallowed. Her head tilted backward. Tears ran down her cheeks. "Okay. Okay. Mikey I'm sorry, but the baby is..."

"It's his." I interrupted. "I know for a fact that you love him like crazy Alicia. You're the best woman that he ever had. Tell him dat its his baby so he can calm down. He hurting right now. He need you." I bucked my eyes and looked into hers. "Tell him Alicia. Tell him."

"Its yours, Mikey. Whose else could it have been? You're the only man I've been with. You're my husband." She cried.

Mikey walked her backward and slammed her into the wall. "Don't you lie to me, bitch. I'll kill you, I swear to God." He cocked the hammer.

I was seconds away from upping my piece and splashing my nigga. I couldn't afford for him to slam my baby mother into the wall anymore. I couldn't risk him putting a bullet into her head. And I couldn't risk her breaking down and exposing our truths to him. There was too much at stake. Before he hurt her, I was going to have to hurt him, unfortunately."

"Please Mikey. Please baby. I love you so freaking much. You are the love of my life. I would die for you. I would never betray you in no way. I'm more of a woman then that." She started to shake. Her knees knocked into each other. Her pregnant belly was poked out under her belly shirt. The belly button was dark brown. She looked vulnerable and it was killing me to not step in. This was my child's mother. Damn their marriage.

"Say shawty, I'ma give you one more chance to tell me what's really good? If you lie to me, I'm putting two in your dome and I'ma cook you in my uncle's cremation oven. You and that baby that I know ain't mine! So, bitch stop playin wit me!"

My hand eased around the handle of my weapon. My trigger finger in place. I envisioned hitting him with at least six slugs. If was going to get at my nigga I was goin to overkill his ass. I had too simply because I had so much love for him.

"Please Mikey. I love you baby. Its your child. I would never do you like that. Phoenix please help me. This ain't right!" Alicia screamed.

He grabbed her neck. "Oh, you think my homeboy gon save yo ass. Bitch ain't nobody can save you. I gave you a chance, but you ain't take it. You can rest in peace wit my mama and my daddy." He threw her against the wall and stood back. Aimed his gun. "Its over!"

I upped my gun. "Mikey nooooooo!"

Boom. Boom. Boom. Boom. Boom.

Chapter 18

The windows shattered all around us as somebody from outside chopped at Mikey and Alicia's crib rapidly. *Thitta-Dat. Thitta-dat. Thitta-dat. Thitta-dat. Thitta-dat. Boom. Boom. Boom. Thitta-dat.* Pictures fell off the walls. Big holes appeared in the walls. A big cloud of smoke covered the interior of the house.

I broke full speed and jumped on top of Alicia. Covered her with my entire body as more and more shots chopped at their place. She was screaming beneath me. I held her tighter. Preparing to feel a slug in any moment now. I had to protect her. I couldn't allow for her to reach harm. I was her only line of defense. She was secretly my child's mother.

Mikey fell on his ass and aimed his gun toward the front of the house and in the direction that the shots were coming from. Then he was firing. *Boo-wa. Boo-wa. Boo-wa.* Boo-wa. *Boo-wa. Boo-wa.* His gun spit round after round.

From the outside the gunfire continued to ensue with no signs of letting up. I stayed on top of Alicia and sort of willed us to the bathroom, throwing a table down to block our path. Once there, I hurriedly placed her in the bath tub. "Shawty stay right here. Stay low and don't get up until I come and get you. You hear me?"

She nodded. More gunfire sounded toward the front of the house. "Thank you, Phoenix. Thank you so much. I love you. I swear I do."

Mikey appeared at the door way, on his knees, holding his shoulder. Blood poured through the cracks of his fingers. "They got me bruh. Them bitch azz niggas got me."

I dropped down low and crawled to the backdoor with my gun out. Slowly, I opened it ran down the steps, and out to the backyard. Once there, I hopped the fence to the neighbor's yard, and ran to the front of their house. I saw the black van parked with the side door opened. In front of it were two masked dudes with Choppers in their hands spitting at the house. On the side of them one dude knelt and lit a cocktail bomb. He stood up and ran toward the front of the house with it.

I aimed at his bitch ass and fired. *Boo*-wa. *Boo*-wa. *Boo*-wa. *Boo*-wa. *Boo*-wa. The gun jumped in my hands, as the rain fell from the sky.

He fell backward and dropped the cocktail. A circle of fire appeared in the street beside his body.

The two masked shooters turned to me and let loose rapidly.

Boom. Boom. Boom. Thitta-dat. Thitta-dat. Thitta-dat. Boom. Boom.

I sent three shots at them and took off running back the way I came.

Before I could make it to the backyard, they were shooting down the gangway. Bullets flew past my head. I could hear them whizzing by one after the next. I got to the backyard and hopped over the fence, then took off running back to the front of the street where the van was parked. The dude that I'd popped was struggling to get to his feet. Blood ran out of the holes in his mid section.

Boo-wa, one to his face. I jumped into the van, just as the shooters were coming from the path that I'd come. They aimed and took fire at me. Their bullets tinkling off the body of the van. I got into the driver's seat as the wind shield shattered and threw the van in drive, storming away from the street. More bullets riddled the van. I drove it two blocks down and crashed it into a pole purposely. I figured that if me and Mikey couldn't catch the people who had targeted his and Alicia's home, then the police would have no trouble doing so. It was petty, but I didn't care. It was survival of the grimiest as far as I was concerned.

When the van made impact with the pole it plunged me forward and threw me out the window. I rolled over the hood, and onto my back. Lightning illuminated the sky. The rain drenched my face. I landed awkwardly. When I went to get up a sharp pain shot up my back, and almost caused me to double over. I fought through it, and jogged with difficulty back to their place, taking the alley the entire way.

***

"Yo, you gotta sit still, Mane. I see the mafuckin bullet. But every time a Bitch try and grab it you get to jumping and shit. Mane sit yo ass still." My cousin Sabrina chastised as she stood over Mikey with a frown on her face. She was a certified nursing assistant, and more than familiar with taking a bullet or two out of a person. I'd never been hit up, but if I had been, she would have been the person I'da went to to get my bullet out of me. Sabrina was my heart, and as country as they came.

"Damn Sabrina. You gotta at least wait until my Perks kick in. This shit hurt like a muthafucka. I feel like crying like a baby. Damn." Mickey wiped the sweat off his forehead. "Say Potna, take my wife out of here upstairs somewhere. I can't let her see me like this."

Sabrina pursed her lips. "I'm sure she'll thank yo tough ass later. Jesus have mercy. Hurry up and get her out of here Phoenix." Sabrina was five feet four inches tall, about one forty, stacked. A red bone, with long curly hair like her little sister Kamya.

161

Alicia stood up holding her stomach. I could tell that she was still rattled by the shooting that had taken pace last night. She'd said very few words ever since then. I was glad that Mikey wanted me to take her upstairs because now I could see how she was going.

"Homeboy I'ma take her to get something to eat. She ain't ate nothing yet. We'll be back in a minute. I gotta check on my shawty too."

He waved me off. "Whatever just go. I gotta get this bullet out of me."

"Mane, your baby wit Kamya and my daddy. She straight. They went to that fair downtown. They ain't supposed to be back until sometime after seven. But she straight doe." Sabrina said, dabbing the cloth filled with alcohol onto Mikey's shoulder.

He jumped and turned the bottle of Patron that he was drinking all the way up. Starting to down it guzzle after guzzle. Sweat slid down the side of his forehead. "Y'all take my truck, Mane. Put some gas in my shit fa me."

Alicia waited until we got outside, and into the truck, before she broke down again. I helped her into the passenger's seat and closed the door behind her.

By the time I hassled around to the driver's seat she appeared to be enraged. She tossed me the keys and beat her fists on the side of her seat. "I hate him now Phoenix. I hate his fuckin guts for what he was getting ready to do to me and my baby." Alicia wrapped her arms protectively around her middle. "It just ain't right. Its not. I'm pregnant I shouldn't have had to go through that shit." She cried in anger.

I started the truck and pulled away from the curb. We drove about twelve blocks in silence. The entire time she was breaking down. The audio of it all was killing me. I

162

hated to hear the mother of my child sound and look so defeated. I knew it was partially my fault. I should have stepped in earlier before he was able to snatch her up and do the things that he did to her. I should've never gotten her pregnant behind his back. As adults she and I should have handled things differently, and from here on out I think we needed to come up with a better plan. It was only right.

"I should've told his ass Phoenix. I should have told him that the baby I'm carrying is yours and got it over with. You wasn't going to let him kill me, was you? Of course not." Alicia answered her own question.

I parked the truck in the parking lot of a Super Walmart and looked over to her. "Alicia, I'm sorry. I should have stepped in ahead of time. I should have never allowed things to go that far. You deserved better than that. I'm sorry lil One."

Alicia nodded. "Its okay. Its not your fault that he's so fucking crazy, or that I married one man, even though I was in love with another." She lowered her head. "What am I going to do? I don't want to be with him anymore Phoenix. I see what he really is, and how he really feels about me and I don't like it. My heart is split. I swear to God that I just wanna be with you. You really care about me."

I held my tongue for a short time. I had a million different things going through my brain. On the one hand I wanted to save and cuff Alicia. I couldn't deny how much I honestly loved and cared about her. I'd felt some type of way about her ever since high school. The only reason I'd never made a move toward her on a serious level is because I knew that I wasn't ready for anything like that. I was unsure if I was ready for it now. I mean there was no doubt in my heart that I would do right by her, but what Alicia expected when she thought in terms if a relationship was monogamy. That was something that I didn't feel I had in me. I was still young, and I had so much of the world to see. I didn't want to be tied down to just one woman right now. At least that's what my mind told me.

"Damn Phoenix, ain't you got nothin to say?" She dabbed at her eyes with a Kleenex from her purse that she'd retrieved from the glove box. "I'm hurting, and I'm so confused right now.

I grabbed her hand and pulled her to the very back of the truck, sat her down and placed my around her. She sat up and removed Mikey's Spring coat that she'd sat on, tossing it on the seat in front of her. Then she snuggled under my arm and laid her head on my shoulder.

I kissed the side of her fore head. "Alicia, I love you. Point blank, and period. But you're married to my right-hand man. Now as bad as you're feeling right now y'all gotta work that out because y'all are together. That's just what it is."

"But I don't want to be with him, Phoenix. This nigga just put a whole ass gun to my head, choked me out and threw me against the wall, all while I'm pregnant. Really? What type of shit is that? Huh?" She shook her head. Tears began to sail down her cheeks again. "That's not love, and Mikey's not stupid. That nigga was getting ready to kill me. He knows this baby isn't his. The dates just don't add up no matter how hard we try to make them do that." Alicia inhaled deeply and blew it out slowly to calm down. "He was going to kill me if that shooting hadn't started Phoenix. He was goin to kill me and you know it."

I saw the entire shooting play out again in my mind's eye. There was no doubt in my mind that if we hadn't been under attack that Mikey would have killed Alicia right before my very eyes. "Damn I know. Fuck, Alicia. So, what do you propose we do? When that nigga finds out that I'm the father of this baby we are going to war, and it will not stop until one of us is six feet under. The homie is a monster, just like me. He bout that life, and murder is human nature to the both of us. I love that nigga. He been my right hand for a long time now."

She jerked her head back and smacked her lips. "Love him? How the hell do you love him so much if you were going behind his back coming at me?"

She pushed me away from her. "You can't have it both ways Phoenix. You gotta be loyal to somebody. You have to choose who you're going to ride for in this equation and then be one hunnit to them. Is it going to be him, or is it going to be me and our unborn child?"

"Shawty, you already know how I am when it comes to my kid. I'll go to the ends of the earth for my baby. Mane, you still ain't answered my question. What do you propose we do?"

"I want us to be together. If we aren't going to be together then I need you to help me break away from him. I hate this man. He could've ended my life, and all for what? Shid, I'm not even so sure that he won't still do it in the very bear future."

"I ain't gon let that happen. Look, for now, just let me stay in bruh's ear. I'll keep his head on straight. You gon continue to chill wit him for a lil while. I'ma get my bread all the way up, and then I'm coming for you. I wish I could do it right now, but I kind of need the homie to go at these Black Haven studs. Plus, it's a whole lot of money to be made. Opportunities can't be squandered. But I'ma get right, make sure you're straight in the process and we'll go from there. That sound like a plan to you?"

She shrugged her shoulders. "I mean what can I do? I ain't got nothin right now. This man controls everything because when we got married that's how he wanted it to be. Me in the kitchen like his fuckin mother, while he controls and handles everything. I'm so stupid."

I pulled her back to me and wrapped my arm around her. "You're not stupid. You were in love, and that's cool. Don't sweat it. I got you. I'ma get you and my baby right. You got my word on that. Just let me know some of the things you need when you need them, and I'll see to it that you have them. Cool?"

She nodded. "Phoenix?"

"Yeah baby?"

"A woman should never be solely dependent on a man. When I break away from Mikey, I'ma be my own boss, you'll see."

I rested my lips against the side of her forehead. "I believe you baby, and I'ma do all that I can to get you right. For now, focus on staying healthy, maintaining that lie, and planning for your future. I'll take care of the rest.

Chapter 19

Instead of us going at Dragon, and his Black Haven niggas right away, we hustled for the next month super hard, and on high alert. Mikey said it was impossible to go at their chin broke when they were moving with so much money. So, we needed to get our scratch back up to compensate for the loss that Dragon had dealt to us, or should I say Mikey, because he hadn't hit my pockets for one red cent. I was the only person that knew where I stashed my shit, and that's how it was always going to be because I didn't trust nobody, not even myself. Orange mound was rocking hard. The lines to our traps were three times as long now, and Nastia always kept us supplied with top notch Rebirth.

Mikey made the hustlers from Brooklyn take turns pulling all nighters in the traps. I did the same thing with Smoke and his crew of eight. There were four men manning the traps at all times while the other four were able to get rest and then they'd switch. I made it a habit to pop up and hustle for eight to ten hours at a time. Then I would be out. I'd hit Link and Jack's pockets as we'd discussed and bounce from the area altogether. Even though I had them on the payroll I still didn't trust them because at the end of the day they were Swine.

On the flip side of everything, me and Mikey, were forming the ultimate plan of attack on Dragon, and his Black Haven boys. Everyday we'd add a little more to the puzzle until things were beginning to look fool proof. I was ready to murder some shit with no regard. I still had not heard from Toya, and I didn't know if she was dead or alive. Like I said before, given the circumstances surrounding everything, I just felt that Dragon and his crew had already taken her out and disposed of the body. But that had yet to be confirmed.

On the fifth day of the fourth week, me and Mikey were coming out of a sub joint right off Broadway. A red bone bitch, with long micro braids, and the side of her head shaved, pulled alongside of my 2020 Escalade rolling a pink drop top Jaguar, and slammed on her brakes. "Say Mane, which one of you fuck niggas is Mikey?" With a mug in her pretty face. She had a red rag around her neck.

Mikey stepped in the street closer to her car. "Bitch I'm Mikey. What it is?"

"Aw, I just wanted to make sho, Playboy. Dis right here is for you." She grabbed a rounded, wrapped present and threw it at his feet. "Nigga, Black Haven will be to holler at you in due time Slime. Suuwoo!" She stepped in the gas pedal and drive off, kicking rocks from the street into the air. She left behind a cloud of smoke.

I jogged into the street, with my hand under my shirt. I mugged her until she made a right at the next intersection. Her tires screeching along the way. "Say I should a popped that lil pretty bitch Potna. Came all the way over here like her balls bugger than ours, Mane."

Mikey waved her off. He knelt in front of the package and picked it up. "Dis mafucka kinda heavy boy. Fuck is it some kind of bomb or something?" He walked around to my passenger's side, and opened the door, sat inside of the truck and got ready to pull the wrapping off.

"Say Mane! Boy what the fuck you doing? Dat could be a bomb or any fuckin thang. You better pay somebody to open that." I hollered, backing away from the truck. I ain't have nothin to prove. If this dumb ass nigga had plans on opening a mysterious package I ain't want no parts of it. His drama wasn't worth dying over some stupidly.

"Bruh its already written when we all gon die. You can't cheat death. Besides these niggas ain't that sophisticated. I just wanna see what the fuck it is."

"Yeah Mane, whatever. Well let me know how that work out for you." I jogged backward. Got to a safe distance that I was still able to see him from.

He tore the wrappings all the way off it. And hollered when he saw what he'd uncovered. His uncle David's head dropped to the sidewalk, and rolled for a second, before it came to a halt.

I covered my mouth with by right hand. "All, hell nall nigga. I know dat ain't who I think it is?"

He got out of the truck and looked down at his uncle's severed head. "I'm tired of dis shit, Durty. Deze niggas been pushing the envelope too much, bruh. Its time to turn all the way up. Erase they ass once and for all. Mafuckas done bodied my parents, and now done took my uncle away from me and shit. Fuck all dis shit, Mane!"

Luckily for us there were only a few people that walked down the block at this time. David's head looked as if it had been stabbed a bunch of times before it was stuffed and wrapped. That was sadistic, and some shit I wouldn't have ever thought about doing.

Mikey picked up the head and got back into the truck with it. "Lets roll Mane. I gotta get some shit in order and we riding out on them fools first thang in the morning. I'm talking the wee hours." He looked over at the head in his lap again.

I jumped in my truck and pulled off. "Any thang you need homeboy I got you. I'm ready to ride on that fully automatic shit. I'm finna get the troops ready. You already know what it is."

"I'ma do the same. Just drop me off at my trap outside the Mound. Let me holler at the Brooklyn Fam and I'ma fuck wit you in a few hours. I gotta put some shit in motion." He continued to look at David's head.

I sighed. "Will do."

***

About twenty minutes later I dropped him off and headed back to Sabrina's crib so I could pick up Shantê. When I got there Sabrina rushed out to, he truck, and jumped into the passenger's seat. "Mane we gotta talk."

I mugged her lil ass. "Shawty you gotta wait. I gotta pick up Shantê so I can drop her off at Kamaya's crib so she can be there when Kamya get off work. I got some shit I'ma have to take care of tonight. I'll fuck wit you later, go and get my daughter." I ordered, nodding toward the house with my head.

"Nall, I don't think you understand. Its some shit that happened that I should have told you a month ago but yo nigga told me not too. He said it wasn't a big deal, but now I know it really is. You might be in danger fucking wit Mikey, Homeboy." She licked her juicy lips, and ran her fingers through her naturally, long, curly hair.

"Danger. What you talking about Sabrina? Every day I step into the slums I'm in danger." I wondered if she was talking about that Black Haven beef? What had she wanted to tell me that Mikey had prevented?

"Say knuckle head, you ain't listening, potna. Look, dat nigga Mikey heard y'all whole ass phone call about a month ago."

"Y'all, who you talking about?" I was confused.

"You and Alicia's. Remember the day I took those bullets out of his shoulder?"

Yeah, what about it?"

"Well that nigga left one of his phones in his truck that day you and Alicia took it to get some gas. That same day, he kept Alicia's phone wit him, and I don't know how it happened, but y'all wound up calling her phone, and he heard y'all talking about their baby supposedly being yours. And how she hated him and wanted to leave him for you. He heard you tell her that you were going to rescue her real soon, and to keep lying about the true father of the baby until you and him finish making some major moves together. Man, that nigga was so heated that he damn near took the bullets out his self afterward."

"What? Why the fuck you just telling me this shit?" I asked ready to slap the taste out of her mouth. What the fuck kind of cousin was she?

"I don't know why I ain't tell you earlier. I wish I had. I'm sorry about that, but that's just what it is right now. What are you going to do? And is that really your baby that Alicia is carrying?"

I was so angry at Sabrina that I imagined myself blowing my cousin's head off her shoulders with no remorse. "Dat ain't yo bidness Sabrina if it is or ain't. You should have told me this shit a long time ago. That nigga could have been smoked me and I wouldn't have been none the wiser. I'm real disappointed in you. Get out my shit, bitch, and tell my daughter to come on. I ain't fuckin wit you for a few days. I though we was better than that. But clearly, I see we ain't. Just be thankful that I ain't knocking yo head off yo shoulders. Bye."

"But... I'm sorry cuz. I know I should have told you, but I just thought y'all should figure that shit out. Y'all been cool for so long and Alicia just pussy. I thought I was supposed to stay in my place. Dats all."

I reached across her lap and pulled open the door. "Bitch get the fuck out my shit and go tell my peoples what I said. Gone."

She tried to grab my arm. "Wait a minute, Phoenix. Don't shit on me like dis. Its my fault, I know, but please cuz. You know we go way back."

I pulled my arm loose and muffed her face. "Get the fuck out my shit. Go. Now."

She fell out of the truck, on to the grass. Got up and looked back at me. "Aiight den Phoenix, well fuck you den. Fuck you and Alicia. I don't care what happen to yo trifling ass." She stormed up the stairs, and into the house.

Minutes later Shantê appeared crying. She slowly came down the steps, taking them one at a time. When she got to the third one, she fell. This really got her to sobbing loudly. I jumped out of my truck to rush and console her. As I was getting out of my truck, two drop top Jaguars were rolling toward Sabrina's house in slow motion. They had two masked shooters in each car sitting in the back seats with assault rifles in their hands. My heart dropped. I looked from them to Shantê, and then it was like everything started to go in slow motion. I pulled both Forty Fives from my waist and started shooting in their direction, just as two more cars turned onto the block from the other direction. My bullets slammed into the windshield of the first car and shattered it.

I continued to buck moving from side to side. "Get on the ground Shantê. Get on the ground!" More bucking, and then I was running to her at full speed. Scooping her in my arms and running along the side of Sabrina's house with my baby in my arms. Bullets whizzed past our heads.

Boom. Boom. Boom. Boom. "Black Haven nigga!" *Boom. Boom. Boom. Boom.*

172

We fell to the ground behind Sabrina's house. I could literally feel the house being rocked from the rapid bullets that assaulted it. Shante screamed loudly in my arms. She shook worse than I'd ever felt her shake before.

A car slammed on its brakes in the alley. I heard doors opening, and guns being cocked. I stood up with Shantê in my arms and took off running as fast as I could. "Hold on baby. Just hold on baby. Just hold on to daddy as tight as you can!

She wrapped her legs around me and tightened her grip along my neck. I scaled one fence with her and then another. Running, knowing that out lives depended on it.

Boom. Boom. Boom. "Get his bitch ass. Shoot! Shoot!" *Boom. Boom. Boom. Boom.*

Another fence. Bullets tinked against the short gate. I held my daughter tighter and kept running. My chest felt as if it was on fire. I could barely breathe but I knew I had to will myself forward. When we got four yards over, I felt like my heart was getting set to burst. The bullets kept on coming. I looked forward and saw a cellar wide open. I imagined somebody had been out in the yard tending the beautiful garden back there and when they heard all the shooting they rushed into the cellar for safety, in doing so they'd left it wide open. I willed myself forward a little more. Got to the cellar and fell to my knees out of breath." Go baby. Go. Please."

More shots were fired in our direction. They kicked up the dirt beside us. I looked behind me and saw people jumping fences with guns in their hands. Shantê pulled at my arm. "Daddy come on. Come on daddy." She fell on her bottom because she was trying to pull me so hard.

I got to my knees and got up. Picked up my baby once again, and ran into the cellar, closed both metal doors.

Bullets slammed into them, putting big dents into the metal. I slid the bar across it to lock the cellar in place.

"Get out of here! Get out of here or I'm going to call the police!" An older white lady screamed, holding a pair of gardening shears in her hands.

"Just stop it lady. Stop it right now! Somebody was shooting at my daddy, and we have to be here!" Shantê yelled with her little fists balled and tears running down her cheeks.

The old lady cocked the big shears back like she was about to attack my baby girl. I stepped in front of Shantê. "Look lady, as soon as all that chaos stops, we'll be out of your hair. We don't want any trouble."

"Just get out! Get out of my fuckin cellar. Now!' She screamed, turning red in the face.

Bomp. Bomp. Bomp. Bomp. It sounded like somebody was trying to beat the doors in. Then the shooting started again. *Boom. Boom. Boom. Boom.*

The old lady fell to her stomach and covered her head. "This is y'all's fault. Help me somebody!"

I laid on top of Shantê while the shooting ensued. It seemed to last for an eternity. Whoever was trying to get a hold of me was angry, and definitely trying to take me out of the game.

Chapter 20

That night I held Shantê in my arms as she shook. Her teeth chattered together. I'd been holding her for a full two hours, and there had still been no change. We were at Kamaya's house, and I was doing all that I could to calm my baby down.

Kamya came out of the kitchen with an apron wrapped around her waist. "'Dinner's ready y'all, its time to put some food in your stomachs." The aroma coming from the kitchen smelled amazing. Like fried chicken, macaroni and cheese, cornbread, and pound cake. Kamya might have only been eighteen years old, but she was a southern woman already. Her cooking skills were second to none.

I loosened my hold on Shantê so I could stand up. She grabbed a hold of my neck even tighter. "Daddy. No. No. Somebody going to try and kill you. Please don't go. Please daddy."

I felt so defeated. I kissed her cheeks. "Baby I'm not going anywhere. We're both going to go in here and eat dinner. You don't have anything to worry about."

She shook her head. "I'm not hungry, but I don't want you to leave me."

Man, I'd never seen my daughter so afraid before. It was the most demoralizing feeling in all the world. I wanted to break down and cry, and at the same time I wanted to murk a million people that had ever hurt a child before.

I sat Shantê on my lap and fed her a little bit of food off my plate. She ate it reluctantly. After we had our fill, she took a bath, and I held her until she fell asleep. Stroking her cheek and kissing her forehead every few minutes. I loved my daughter with everything I had inside of me.

Ghost

After I put her to bed, I jumped in the shower and washed the day's poison off me. I didn't know what I was going to do, or how I was going to handle things with Mikey. I didn't know if I should come clean to him about Alicia and I, or if I should just see how he would play things down the road. I knew that this option would be the most dangerous. Mikey was a loose cannon. He had the ability to snap out about things out of the blue. That's what I wanted to avoid. Him snapping out could have meant death for me, Alicia, Shantê, or my unborn child. I just had no way of knowing. On the other hand, maybe coming to him like a man would soften the blow that was sure to come. I didn't fear Mikey. No, not at all. He was my homeboy. Had he been any other nigga, I would have knocked his head off and kept it moving. Life was too short to live in paranoia. I didn't like worrying about anybody doing something to me. I felt that the easiest way to avoid paranoia of an enemy was to get rid of them by any means necessary. Mikey got the benefit of the doubt because he was like my brother, as cliché as that may have seemed.

At the conclusion of my shower. Kamya came into the bathroom and dried my body from head to toe, while I stood in front of her naked. "Phoenix you need to feel lucky that you and my lil cousin are alive. I don't know what the fuck is going on, but I can't stand to lose you. I love you so fuckin much." She dropped the towel and kissed my lips hard as she hugged my body to hers. "Damn."

I slowly wrapped my arms around her body and rested my lips on her forehead. That was a habit of mine. "That's why I gotta kill them niggas, shawty. I been ducking these fuck boys for way too long trying my best to let Mikey run the show because he had all the plugs. Dat shit over wit now though. I'm finna run shit. I'm finna get rid of these

176

Black Haven niggas, and then me and Mikey need to sit down and get an understanding. We can't get rich with him running shit, or there being bad blood between us. Somethin gotta shake."

Kamya lowered her head. "Is it true that Alicia carrying your baby?" She whispered.

I shrugged my shoulders. "It might be, I mean we have fucked around a lot, and the dates add up. If it is I ain't got no choice other than to do the right thing."

Kamya smacked her lips. She pushed me off her. "Damn Phoenix. I can see you fucking her a few times, but pregnant? Man, what the fuck? I ain't enough for you or something?" She turned her back to me.

I pinched the top of my nose and exhaled. Slid behind her and pulled her back to my body. "Kamya, me and her was fuckin around way before you and I was. Besides all that, you're my blood, shawty. You know can't shit good come from what we're doing. Pretty soon it has to come to an end."

"An end?" She turned around and faced me. "What the fuck are you talking about, Phoenix? I love you. I gotta be with you. This ain't no you and Sabrina type of shit. This is my whole ass heart we're talking about. You can't just sever things when you're ready to. That's not fair cuz. I'm a long way from being able to do that." She slid her arms onto my shoulders and laid her head on my chest. "Do you love me?"

I nodded. "Yeah Kamya, I love you. You're my baby."

"Nall Phoenix. I'm not talking that family love shit. I mean do you honestly love and care for me as a man would a woman?" She looked into my eyes. "The truth baby, because I'm crazy about you. I don't care how silly I may sound, and I don't care about our being related either. I

177

don't want us to be labeled as anything when we look at each other if it isn't male and female. So, do you really love me?"

I brushed her pretty hair out of her face and fixed it so that it stayed behind her ears. "Yeah Kamya, I love you as a woman. You are my baby, and there is nothin in this world that I wouldn't do for you, shawty. You should already know that."

She smiled. "I do."

"Kamya but we can not be together in that way that you want to because you are my cou--." I started.

She pressed her finger to my lips. "Ssh, this is Memphis, Phoenix. Damn near every household down here doing what we doing. You're just over thinking things. Just trace our family's history." She took her finger away from my lips and sucked it into her mouth. "I need you right now. I need you to lay me down, and to fuck me good. My lil pussy getting wet from just thanking about it right now. Huh feel." She slid my fingers into her panties and rubbed them over her bald pussy lips. They were meaty and hot. My middle finger slid into her tight hole. Her lips wrapped around it "Unnnn, yes." She placed her foot on top of the tub.

I added a second digit and got to fingering her pussy her wet pussy at full speed. I sucked on her neck and cuffed her perfect titties through her white tee shirt. Her nipples were stiff as erasers. I sucked them one at a time.

"Yes. Yes. Phoenix. Yes. Gimme some cuz. Gimme some of that dick, you got me so horney fo yo ass." She dropped down, and wrapped her little fist around my stalk, stroking it up and down. Kamya put the head into her mouth and sucked hard on it. She was deep throating me as far as she could take it and gagging along the way.

Duffle Bag Cartel

I pulled her up. "Bend yo ass over that toilet. Come on."
She stuck her ass into the air and held on to the back of
the toilet. 'Fuck me, cuz. Put all that dick inside of me,
please." She begged sucking on her bottom lip.

I ran the big head in between her sex lips, and pushed
it home, sliding all the way in. Kamya arched her back and
moaned. I rubbed all over that fat ass before going to work,
long stroking her at full speed. Her ass crashed into my lap,
jiggling and shaking. That pussy was hot as lava, and soft
as cotton.

"Uh! Phoenix. Yes. Yes. Fuck me. Harder. Harder. Aw
fuck!"

I closed my eyes and kept on pounding, while holding
her little hips. I was trying to hit her soft bottom. I felt a
draft on my ankles. The door creaked, causing me to open
my eyes. Before I could react, it was too late. I felt the cold
steel pressed to the back of my neck.

Kamya continued to moan loudly, unaware of the in-
truder.

"You bitch ass nigga, I can't believe you. You gon do
this to me." He pressed the gun harder into the back of my
head. "You gon fuck my wife and get her pregnant. This
the last piece of pussy you gon ever get!" Mikey growled,
causing Kamya to scream at the top of her lungs.

To Be Continued...
Duffle Bag Cartel 2
Coming Soon

Submission Guideline

Submit the first three chapters of your completed manuscript to ldpsubmissions@gmail.com, subject line: Your book's title. The manuscript must be in a .doc file and sent as an attachment. Document should be in Times New Roman, double spaced and in size 12 font. Also, provide your synopsis and full contact information. If sending multiple submissions, they must each be in a separate email.

Have a story but no way to send it electronically? You can still submit to LDP/Ca$h Presents. Send in the first three chapters, written or typed, of your completed manuscript to:

LDP: Submissions Dept
Po Box 870494
Mesquite, Tx 75187

DO NOT send original manuscript. Must be a duplicate.

Provide your synopsis and a cover letter containing your full contact information.

Thanks for considering LDP and Ca$h Presents.

Duffle Bag Cartel

Coming Soon from Lock Down Publications/Ca$h Presents

BOW DOWN TO MY GANGSTA

By **Ca$h**

TORN BETWEEN TWO

By **Coffee**

BLOOD STAINS OF A SHOTTA **III**

By **Jamaica**

STEADY MOBBIN **III**

By **Marcellus Allen**

BLOOD OF A BOSS **V**

By **Askari**

LOYAL TO THE GAME **IV**

LIFE OF SIN II

By **T.J. & Jelissa**

A DOPEBOY'S PRAYER **II**

By **Eddie "Wolf" Lee**

IF LOVING YOU IS WRONG… **III**

LOVE ME EVEN WHEN IT HURTS **II**

By **Jelissa**

TRUE SAVAGE **VII**

By **Chris Green**

BLAST FOR ME **III**

A BRONX TALE III

DUFFLE BAG CARTEL II

By **Ghost**

ADDICTIED TO THE DRAMA **III**

Ghost

By **Jamila Mathis**
LIPSTICK KILLAH **III**
WHAT BAD BITCHES DO **III**
KILL ZONE **II**
By **Aryanna**
THE COST OF LOYALTY **II**
By **Kweli**
SHE FELL IN LOVE WITH A REAL ONE **II**
By **Tamara Butler**
RENEGADE BOYS **III**
By **Meesha**
CORRUPTED BY A GANGSTA **IV**
By **Destiny Skai**
A GANGSTER'S CODE **III**
By **J-Blunt**
KING OF NEW YORK IV
RISE TO POWER II
By **T.J. Edwards**
GORILLAS IN THE BAY II
De'Kari
THE STREETS ARE CALLING II
Duquie Wilson
KINGPIN KILLAZ III
Hood Rich
STEADY MOBBIN' **III**
Marcellus Allen
SINS OF A HUSTLA II

182

Duffle Bag Cartel

ASAD

TRIGGADALE II

Elijah R. Freeman

MARRIED TO A BOSS 2...

By Destiny Skai & Chris Green

KINGS OF THE GAME II

Playa Ray

<u>Available Now</u>

<u>RESTRAINING ORDER **I & II**</u>

By **CA$H & Coffee**

<u>LOVE KNOWS NO BOUNDARIES **I II & III**</u>

By **Coffee**

<u>RAISED AS A GOON I, II, III & IV</u>

<u>BRED BY THE SLUMS I, II, III</u>

<u>BLAST FOR ME I & II</u>

<u>ROTTEN TO THE CORE I III</u>

<u>A BRONX TALE I, II</u>

<u>DUFFLE BAG CARTEL</u>

By **Ghost**

<u>LAY IT DOWN **I & II**</u>

<u>LAST OF A DYING BREED</u>

<u>BLOOD STAINS OF A SHOTTA I & II</u>

By **Jamaica**

<u>LOYAL TO THE GAME</u>

<u>LOYAL TO THE GAME II</u>

LOYAL TO THE GAME III

LIFE OF SIN

By **TJ & Jelissa**

BLOODY COMMAS I & II

SKI MASK CARTEL I II & III

KING OF NEW YORK I II,III

RISE TO POWER

By **T.J. Edwards**

IF LOVING HIM IS WRONG…I & II

LOVE ME EVEN WHEN IT HURTS

By **Jelissa**

WHEN THE STREETS CLAP BACK I & II III

By **Jibril Williams**

A DISTINGUISHED THUG STOLE MY HEART I II & III

LOVE SHOULDN'T HURT I II III

RENEGADE BOYS I & II

By **Meesha**

A GANGSTER'S CODE I & II

By **J-Blunt**

PUSH IT TO THE LIMIT

By **Bre' Hayes**

BLOOD OF A BOSS **I, II, III & IV**

By **Askari**

THE STREETS BLEED MURDER **I, II & III**

THE HEART OF A GANGSTA I II& III

By **Jerry Jackson**

CUM FOR ME

CUM FOR ME 2

CUM FOR ME 3

CUM FOR ME 4

An **LDP Erotica Collaboration**

BRIDE OF A HUSTLA **I II & II**

THE FETTI GIRLS **I, II& III**

CORRUPTED BY A GANGSTA I, II & III

By **Destiny Skai**

WHEN A GOOD GIRL GOES BAD

By **Adrienne**

A GANGSTER'S REVENGE **I II III & IV**

THE BOSS MAN'S DAUGHTERS

THE BOSS MAN'S DAUGHTERS II

THE BOSSMAN'S DAUGHTERS III

THE BOSSMAN'S DAUGHTERS IV

THE BOSS MAN'S DAUGHTERS **V**

A SAVAGE LOVE **I & II**

BAE BELONGS TO ME

A HUSTLER'S DECEIT I, II

WHAT BAD BITCHES DO I, II

By **Aryanna**

A KINGPIN'S AMBITON

A KINGPIN'S AMBITION **II**

I MURDER FOR THE DOUGH

By **Ambitious**

TRUE SAVAGE

TRUE SAVAGE II

TRUE SAVAGE III

TRUE SAVAGE IV

TRUE SAVAGE V

TRUE SAVAGE VI

By **Chris Green**

A DOPEBOY'S PRAYER

By **Eddie "Wolf" Lee**

THE KING CARTEL **I, II & III**

By **Frank Gresham**

THESE NIGGAS AIN'T LOYAL **I, II & III**

By **Nikki Tee**

GANGSTA SHYT **I II &III**

By **CATO**

THE ULTIMATE BETRAYAL

By **Phoenix**

BOSS'N UP **I , II & III**

By **Royal Nicole**

I LOVE YOU TO DEATH

By Destiny J

I RIDE FOR MY HITTA

I STILL RIDE FOR MY HITTA

By **Misty Holt**

LOVE & CHASIN' PAPER

By **Qay Crockett**

TO DIE IN VAIN

SINS OF A HUSTLA

Duffle Bag Cartel

By **ASAD**

BROOKLYN HUSTLAZ

By **Boogsy Morina**

BROOKLYN ON LOCK I & II

By **Sonovia**

GANGSTA CITY

By **Teddy Duke**

A DRUG KING AND HIS DIAMOND I & II III

A DOPEMAN'S RICHES

HER MAN, MINE'S TOO I, II

CASH MONEY HO'S

By **Nicole Goosby**

TRAPHOUSE KING **I II & III**

KINGPIN KILLAZ

By **Hood Rich**

LIPSTICK KILLAH **I, II**

CRIME OF PASSION I & II

By **Mimi**

STEADY MOBBN' **I, II**

By **Marcellus Allen**

WHO SHOT YA **I, II**

Renta

GORILLAZ IN THE BAY

DE'KARI

TRIGGADALE

Elijah R. Freeman

GOD BLESS THE TRAPPERS I, II, III

THESE SCANDALOUS STREETS I, II, III

FEAR MY GANGSTA I, II, III

THESE STREETS DON'T LOVE NOBODY I, II

BURY ME A G I, II, III, IV, V

Tranay Adams

THE STREETS ARE CALLING

Duquie Wilson

MARRIED TO A BOSS...

By Destiny Skai & Chris Green

KINGS OF THE GAME II

Playa Ray

BOOKS BY LDP'S CEO, CA$H

TRUST IN NO MAN

TRUST IN NO MAN 2

TRUST IN NO MAN 3

BONDED BY BLOOD

SHORTY GOT A THUG

THUGS CRY

THUGS CRY 2

THUGS CRY 3

TRUST NO BITCH

TRUST NO BITCH 2

TRUST NO BITCH 3

TIL MY CASKET DROPS

RESTRAINING ORDER

RESTRAINING ORDER 2

IN LOVE WITH A CONVICT

Coming Soon

BONDED BY BLOOD 2

BOW DOWN TO MY GANGSTA

Ghost

CPSIA information can be obtained
at www.ICGtesting.com
Printed in the USA
LVHW020613080520
654924LV00002B/206